A Candlelight Ecstasy Romance ®

**"EVERY GOOD THING HAS TO END,
PRINCESS." RHYS'S
DEEP VOICE BROUGHT HER BACK TO
THE PRESENT.**

"Must you be such a party-pooper?" she asked
dreamily.

Rhys made no effort to move his large body
that was still keeping her pressed deep into the
cushions. He did shift his position enough to
wedge one fist beneath her chin as he regarded
her with amusement. "Little girls shouldn't play
with fire, princess. All sorts of accidents can happen."

"I wouldn't call what happened between us an
accident, Rhys," she whispered. "Would you?"

A CANDLELIGHT ECSTASY ROMANCE ®

BEGUILED BY A STRANGER

Eleanor Woods

A CANDLELIGHT ECSTASY ROMANCE ®

Published by
Dell Publishing Co., Inc.
1 Dag Hammarskjold Plaza
New York, New York 10017

ISBN: 0–440–10496–3

Printed in the United States of America

First printing—May 1984

To Our Readers:

We have been delighted with your enthusiastic response to Candlelight Ecstasy Romances®, and we thank you for the interest you have shown in this exciting series.

In the upcoming months we will continue to present the distinctive sensuous love stories you have come to expect only from Ecstasy. We look forward to bringing you many more books from your favorite authors and also the very finest work from new authors of contemporary romantic fiction.

As always, we are striving to present the unique, absorbing love stories that you enjoy most—books that are more than ordinary romance.

Your suggestions and comments are always welcome. Please write to us at the address below.

Sincerely,

The Editors
Candlelight Romances
1 Dag Hammarskjold Plaza
New York, New York 10017

BEGUILED
BY A
STRANGER

CHAPTER ONE

"So, gentlemen, as you've been shown today in our presentation, our community can offer you everything your company has been looking for. And I assure you we'll be more than happy to accommodate you in any way, should you decide to locate here. Now"—the slender, brunette flashed her warmest smile at the group of men seated at the long conference table—"not only are we hoping to impress you with our community, but we're also going to attempt to bribe you by serving you an excellent lunch."

With all the confidence of one who has just successfully pulled off an unbelievable coup, Megan Colby quickly gathered up the material used in her talk and returned it to the taupe-colored, soft leather briefcase. This break in what had been a hectic morning gave her a brief moment to observe surreptitiously the expressions on the faces of the five visitors who represented a large company that specialized in casual wear for adults and children, their most popular item being jeans. Megan had been working for over six months with this particular day in mind. Now that it had almost become a reality, she found herself rather heady with the excitement of the moment.

The arrival of Corbet Industries, if she could actually nail them down to agreeing to establish a plant on the Florida coast, would certainly go a long way toward silencing certain members of Coastal's board who had attended this meeting and had been against Megan's hiring from the start.

"You were fantastic, Megan," Jack Lindsey murmured close to her ear as she moved from her position at the head of the table and began edging her way toward the door of the adjoining room where lunch was to be served. "I'm sure I don't have to tell you that you've ruined Jerome Kennedy's lunch, do I?"

Megan gave Jack a sideways glance, her full, attractive mouth curving into a knowing grin. "Indeed, you don't. He and several other members were more hopeful of seeing me fall flat on my face, figuratively speaking, than of securing Corbet Industries for this area."

She raised one forefinger and pushed at the nosepiece of the tan-framed glasses she wore. It would have taken more than the glasses, however, to hide the sparkle in the blue eyes that were thickly fringed by dark lashes. There was a certain satisfaction in her face, from the smooth forehead and softly arched brows to the small, straight nose and determined chin.

Jack laid a friendly hand on her shoulder and gave her a quick squeeze. "Forget their long faces. They're just jealous. Especially Jerome. His son was a miserable failure in the same position you now hold, so I suppose it's difficult for him to admit that you're doing a better job."

"Because I'm a woman, you mean," Megan ruefully concurred. "I suppose I'd be foolish to expect a simple word of thanks for a job well done. Because I am a woman, and if Corbet will settle here, it will cause the battle lines to be even more firmly drawn."

"Don't let it bother you," Jack hastened to assure her. "There are enough members on our side to successfully squash any attempt to sabotage this latest venture. By the way"—he smiled down at her—"are you free for dinner this evening?"

"As a matter of fact I am," Megan told him.

"Great. Shall I pick you up around seven?"

"I'll be ready." By then they were entering the banquet room and Megan spied Rita Clay, the owner of the catering service, hired to cater the important lunch. "Excuse me, Jack, but I need to speak to Rita. I'll see you later." With a quick smile thrown over her shoulder she made her way toward the attractive, middle-aged woman supervising the bustling waiters.

"Everything running on schedule, Rita?" Megan asked.

"Couldn't be better, so stop worrying. Everything on that seafood platter is fresh," the older woman assured her. "You know I wouldn't let you down."

"Thanks, Rita," Megan sighed. "I sound like a mother hen with a bunch of baby chicks, don't I."

"Well . . ." Rita began rather dryly. "When you're dealing with men, honey, they often give you that impression. They like to have us believe that the world would stop turning without their intervention, while you and I know it would probably run a lot smoother without them."

Megan chuckled at the blonde's cryptic description of men in general. "They do have their uses, though, don't you agree?"

"Perhaps. But don't let it get out that I said so," Rita grudgingly admitted.

The luncheon went off without a hitch, and Megan spent the remainder of the afternoon with Josh Rabin and the other four that made up the delegation. They made another tour of the large, sprawling facility that Megan hoped would soon be bustling with activity.

By late afternoon Megan had Josh's word that Corbet Industries would indeed locate a plant on the suggested site.

As Megan drove her guests to the local airport and their waiting company jet, she found herself physically and emotionally exhausted. Once the plane was airborne, she got back into her car and

14

drove to her apartment, looking forward to a long soak in a warm tub before her dinner date with Jack.

Sometime later, as she relaxed amid a frothy warmth of bubbles and water, a tightly folded towel supporting her head, Megan took the time to lazily reflect on her career, past and present.

She'd known early in life that a job from nine to five, of being stuck in an office with typing and shorthand as her main duties, would never do for her. Megan had been raised in a family made up entirely of men. She was the youngest to four brothers. She'd been affectionately called "runt" by her older siblings, although very little consideration had been offered because of her sex, nor had she expected any.

Her mother's death, when she was two years old, hadn't been the heart-wrenching experience for Megan that it was for her dad and brothers. Consequently, her childhood was in some respects different from her friends', but certainly not lacking in love and attention. When she was twelve her dad's sister was suddenly widowed and came to keep house for the Colby clan.

Rather than attempting to smother her niece with a sudden gush of mother love, Beatrice Lange encouraged the young girl to seek her fullest potential in life, and not necessairly conform to what was commonly expected of a woman. After graduation from college with a degree in business, Megan landed a position with a large economic development foundation in South Carolina.

Her major responsibility was to coordinate the visits of prospective clients to certain areas and to work with the business leaders in the community to assure that the presentation was geared to attracting industry.

From there she went back to Atlanta as an assistant to the city planner, and finally to her present position as head of the Coastal Industrial Development Foundation.

As she raised one shapely, tanned leg and leisurely soaped the smooth skin, Megan knew that her accomplishment of the day would in no way enhance her credibility with certain members of the board who disliked her. But it would certainly cause them to look elsewhere to throw their usual asinine criticisms . . . at least for a few weeks.

When the doorbell sounded at exactly four minutes to seven, Megan scooped up her envelope-style purse and went to answer the door.

"You look gorgeous," Jack told her as he took in the camisole bodice with inserts of lace and the flounced skirt of the white dress that perfectly reflected her tan.

"Thank you," Megan smiled. "You're looking nice as well, I think," she said to the hazy outline of his face and body.

Jack gave a resigned sigh, then reached for her hand. "It's going to be one of those evenings, huh?" He reached beyond her, grasped the doorknob, and closed the door. "I've told you a million times that you're the sexiest gal I've ever seen wearing glasses."

"Which means nothing," Megan replied airily as she transferred her hand from his firm grip to the crook of his elbow. "I bet you've never even dated a girl who wore glasses."

"Oh, no, you don't," he laughed as they made their way to his waiting car. "I refuse to fall into that trap again. Just suffice it to say that I find nothing objectionable about you with or without your glasses, Miss Colby."

"How nicely put, Mr. Lindsey." She grinned cheekily. "Somehow I was certain I could count on you to come up with the right answer."

Jack seated her in the car, then walked around and got in behind the steering wheel. "I'm not so sure I like the sound of complacency that edged your compliment," he remarked ruefully, giving her a sharp look laced with a frown as he started the engine and drove away.

Megan let her head drop back against the seat and fondly regarded him. "It *was* meant as a compliment, and you know it."

Jack squeezed her hand which rested on the seat between them. "Why don't you accept the proposals of marriage I've been offering you for the past six months instead of showering me with kind words?"

"Because, you idiot, we both know it would be a terrible mistake. We're too good friends to ruin it all by marrying." There was a light, teasing lilt in her voice, but underneath it all, Megan knew she'd never spoken truer words.

Jack was handsome and fun to be with. His family was in banking, and he had slipped neatly into the role expected of him. And even though there were moments when he had excited her with his kisses, she still held back, some sixth sense warning her that her acquiescence toward deepening the relationship would only wind up hurting him.

There was something missing in Jack's makeup that she couldn't quite put her finger on, some spark, some mysterious force without which she was unable to love him.

She'd often thought it silly to place such significance on this tiny flaw in Jack's personality, but she did nevertheless. Perhaps flaw wasn't the correct word, Megan thought fleetingly. The flaw lay within her, for wanting the stars to shoot across the sky and bells to ring when she met the man of her dreams. She was twenty-nine years old and still waiting. What if all the waiting had been in vain? What if there were no such things as shooting stars and bells sounding?

Dinner with Jack was always perfect, and this evening was no exception. He was a master at keeping a lively conversation going, and Megan wasn't bored for a single moment.

She was sitting back in her chair, laughing at a particular amusing story, when she heard Jack give a low murmur of surprise.

"What is it?" Megan asked as she idly traced

the delicate pattern on the stem of her wineglass with one slender forefinger.

"It's not a what, it's Rhys Warner. He's been in the bank a couple of times this week."

"Oh? He sounds important. Is he?"

"Well now, that depends," Jack drawled teasingly.

"On what?"

"Whether or not one is impressed with a self-made millionaire and a hell of a nice guy to boot."

"You sound as though you really like this character."

There was a subtle arching of Jack's brows, and for a moment Megan thought she saw regret skitter across his face. But the glow of the candle was dim and she couldn't quite trust her eyes. Yet nothing could disguise the quiet longing in his voice when he spoke.

"I do like him. He's one of those unique men the rest of us poor fools would give our eyeteeth to be like. He reminds me of a gambler whose fortune hangs on a single roll of the dice. You know instinctively he'll throw the dice without blinking an eye . . . and win."

"Always?"

"Oh, yes. The Rhys Warners of this world refuse to accept anything but complete victory."

"Then I sincerely hope our paths never cross," Megan said softly, a peculiar shiver sweeping over her. "He sounds overwhelming. And in case you've forgotten, I was raised with four overbearing brothers."

Once again Jack looked past her, an amused grin touching his lips. "Hmm, the next few minutes should prove interesting, Megan; Rhys Warner is headed this way. Short of hiding under the table, I can see no way out of introducing the two of you."

Before she could formulate a successful put-down, Megan felt the hair on her nape literally stand on end. She took a deep breath and held it. She felt foolish and at the same time frightened of a man she'd never met, never even heard of until five minutes ago.

The next thing she was aware of was Jack rising to his feet, his hand outstretched and a smile on his face. "Rhys, nice to see you. I'd like for you to meet a friend of mine, Megan Colby . . . Rhys Warner."

Until that moment Megan had kept her head averted. With an expression of casual curiosity shielding her features, she looked up into a face that despite the fuzziness of her vision caught and held her full attention. His features hinted of strength and determination, and she didn't need her glasses to distinguish the darkness of his hair, the hawkish line of his nose, and the stubborn set of his chin and jaw.

"Miss Colby," came a deep voice that caused the beat of her heart to skip erratically.

"Mr. Warner," Megan quietly responded. Good heavens, she was thinking to herself as she heard Jack invite Rhys Warner to join them, and his acceptance, no wonder Jack was impressed and rightfully so. This was a man who was miscast in the present. He exuded an aura of excitement that had Megan picturing him on a ship's deck, a cutlass strapped on his hip. He was tall, and appeared utterly ruthless.

Now that he was seated to her right, she was only slightly more able to discern his features. She found herself inordinately curious as to the color of his eyes. But short of coming out and asking, she had no choice but to guess. Of all times to leave her glasses behind, Megan fretted.

"Is Pensacola your home, Miss Colby, or are you vacationing here?" this disturbing newcomer asked.

"Megan is head of our Coastal I.D. operation, Rhys," Jack spoke up. "We were very fortunate to get her. She can be mighty persuasive when it comes to convincing new industries to locate in the area."

"Really," Rhys said pleasantly. Though there was nothing overt in his voice or in his gaze that was fully trained on her, Megan caught the undercurrents of ridicule emanating from him and immediately became defensive.

"What about you, Mr. Warner? Are you on vacation?" she asked briskly, missing altogether the flash of amusement from Jack at the shortness of her question.

"In a manner of speaking," Rhys replied non-committally. "I'm always on the lookout for an

21

area with a potential for expansion to invest in. Would you recommend this area, Miss Colby?"

"That would depend, Mr. Warner, on exactly what your line of investment is. Are you interested from the manufacturer's point of view or from the speculative angle?"

"Both. Lodestar Inc. is an umbrella concern. Our holdings are quite diversified," he smoothly corrected her. "Perhaps you could show me around while I'm here, Miss Colby."

"As you say, Mr. Warner, perhaps. If you'd like, you can call my office and set up an appointment. I'll be out of town several days next week, so if not on this visit, then maybe the next time you're in town we can get together."

"Oh, we will, Miss Colby," Rhys Warner was quick to agree. "We definitely will get together. Now"—he looked from Megan to Jack, a pleased smile on his face—"if you will excuse me, the people I'm having dinner with have just arrived."

After Rhys had gone, Jack looked at Megan and grinned. "I take it you weren't impressed with Rhys Warner?"

"Physically he's very attractive—what I could see of him, that is. Otherwise, I don't think I care for him. I got the distinct impression he considers me as nothing more than a figurehead while someone else does the actual work. Show him around, indeed! He made it sound as though I were in charge of the local Welcome Wagon."

"Tsk, tsk," Jack chuckled. "He really did rub you the wrong way."

22

Megan shrugged, and found that she really didn't want to discuss Rhys Warner at all. His presence had been very disturbing and she was at a loss to understand why.

She wasn't some naive young thing ready to drop everything and fall all over him simply because of his wealth and position. There'd been too many battles she'd had to fight with men who had personality traits similar to Rhys Warner's for her to allow him to belittle her capabilities. On the other hand, she found her emotional reaction to him puzzling. She felt almost betrayed by the uncertainty she'd felt in his presence.

"Now, I wonder why Jerome Kennedy and his worthless son, Tom, are having dinner with Rhys?" Jack broke into the momentary lull in the conversation.

"You're kidding!" Megan exclaimed, itching to turn around and stare.

"Not at all. They've even brought Stacy Owens as window dressing." He continued to give her a play-by-play. "She's looking very sexy in her tight black dress that seems to be missing some vital pieces of material in the area of her ample cleavage," he finished disconsolately.

"Draw in your tongue, Jack, you're drooling." Megan couldn't help but laugh. "I wonder what Stacy sees in Tom? She is with Tom, isn't she?"

"It appears so." Jack sighed wistfully. He looked at Megan and briefly closed his eyes. "Just think of it . . . all her, er, charms wasted on that creep."

"What you're really saying is that it should be you she's wasting herself on," Megan teased.

"Of course," he stated loftily. "I'm a much nicer person than Tom. I can do a great deal more for Miss Owens than her current escort."

"Oh, I'm sure you can, Jack. But I somehow don't think it's her modeling career you have in mind." Megan gave him a disgusted look. "Stacy is a nice kid. A little anxious to succeed, but then, aren't we all? As for you, you wimp, you're as bad as Tom Kennedy."

"I'm wounded." Jack eyed her with a teasing glint in his blue eyes.

"You're also well on your way toward becoming what is distastefully referred to as a dirty old man."

"Old?" he croaked, his mouth gaping like a fish. "Thirty-nine is considered by most women to be an excellent year. Smooth and mellow, but with enough age to be mysterious."

"There's no mystery about being oversexed, Jack." Megan stared steadily at him. "You don't need Stacy Owens's youthful charms; you need a doctor."

"Damn! But you're cruel." He struggled to appear highly insulted, then gave in to the laughter threatening to choke him.

Unbeknownst to either of them, several heads turned and stared with amused indulgence at the attractive couple, particularly Rhys Warner.

His gaze narrowed considerably as he watched Megan, her profile thrown into gentle relief by

24

the candle in the hurricane holder in the center of the table. There was a creamy softness about her skin that appealed to him. His dark eyes lingered on the graceful arch of her neck and shoulders.

He wondered exactly what her relationship was with Jack Lindsey. Were they lovers? A dark frown appeared on his broad brow as that thought flashed through his mind. Megan Colby had piqued his interest, and he didn't like to think of her being involved with another man. But even if she was, Rhys didn't feel threatened. Women were the same the world over.

He hadn't been fooled in the least by her coolness. He'd seen that same trick used over and over again, and it always meant the same thing. A sophisticated little game of chase, ending with him catching the willing victim.

It suddenly dawned on him that he was annoyed with Megan for attempting to employ this same ruse. He hoped she would show more originality as their relationship progressed, as he was sure it would.

With an inaudible sigh of boredom easing past his lips, Rhys turned and cast his most charming smile upon Stacy Owens, his dark eyes as cold as ice.

Later that evening, as Megan prepared for bed, there was a pensiveness about her as she thought back over the day, the evening, and lastly, Rhys Warner.

While Lodestar Inc. wasn't an everyday, household word, she knew that in financial circles it meant power and stability. She'd also read somewhere of the complicated structure within the corporation wherein its founder was in complete control, the founder being Rhys Warner.

Megan slipped into bed and pulled the sheet and light blanket up to her shoulders. Would he really call and make an appointment to see her? An even more curious question caught at her. Would she see him?

CHAPTER TWO

Megan arrived at her office the next morning knowing that the day wasn't likely to end before seven or eight o'clock that evening. Having Corbet Industries agree to locate in the area was only half the battle. The paperwork and meetings to follow would be staggering.

"Good morning, Katie." Megan smiled cheerfully at the dark-haired secretary. "How's it looking so far?"

Katie Lumas smiled, then drew the appointment book forward. She thoughtfully tapped it with one finger, then looked up at Megan. "Busy. That presentation you'll need for your trip next week has to be completed. As per your instructions I've set up a meeting for eleven o'clock today with the board to discuss the issuance of Industrial Development bonds to buy the new

27

equipment for Corbet. That takes care of the morning. The afternoon looks to be busy as well." She handed a neat stack of telephone messages to Megan. "None of these seemed urgent other than a Mr. Rhys Warner. He's already called three times."

"Well." Megan skeptically eyed her friend. "You really know how to brighten a gal's day, don't you? I'd planned on working late, but not all night," she quipped, waving the slips of paper in her hand.

"Can't argue with success." Katie grinned. "Congratulations, Megan. That was quite a deal you pulled off yesterday."

"Thanks, Katie. But you played a large part in that moment of victory as well. Let's just hope my trip to Atlanta will be as successful."

"Stop worrying, it will be. Besides, you've accomplished more in the one year you've been here than Tom Kennedy did in four."

"Which doesn't sit well at all with the elder Mr. Kennedy," Megan ruefully reasoned. "A person could almost become paranoid with the Messrs. Kennedy and cronies, and their habit of casting an evil eye on every single thing this foundation does." She pushed herself upright. "By the way, Katie, Josh Rabin asked for a general labor survey within a thirty-mile radius. See that the business leaders in the supporting towns get the forms. We'll also need a more specific survey of women suited for the garment industry, between the ages of eighteen and forty-five."

"Will do, boss," Katie replied, reaching for the top drawer of the lateral file cabinet to her right.

Megan turned and walked into her own office and closed the door. After placing her purse in a desk drawer and dropping the briefcase on her desk, she sat down in the soft leather chair and thoughtfully thumbed through the messages Katie had given her.

She stared at Rhys Warner's name, remembering the quiet ripple of apprehension that had washed over her when introduced to him. She also was reminded of the subtle ridicule in his voice and the self-assured manner he'd put forth when he talked to her.

With annoyance bracketing her lips, Megan calmly ripped his messages in half and let them float from her slender fingers toward the waste basket.

"Choose someone else to act as your guide, Mr. Warner," she muttered beneath her breath. "I've more important things to do with my time."

After looking over the remainder of the messages and arranging them by order of their importance, she reached for the receiver, placed a call to the courthouse and asked for Amelia Wrafton.

As soon as the elderly lady answered, Megan could tell she was upset. Once the social amenities were dispensed with, Megan asked if there was some problem she could help with.

"Oh, my dear, I hope so," Amelia wailed. "I've just learned of the most dreadful thing."

"I'm sorry, Amelia," Megan answered consolingly. She'd learned from past experience that getting information from Amelia could be an arduous task. One simply had to wait until that spry, birdlike individual was ready to divulge her latest crisis.

"There should be a law against people who give their word and then conveniently forget about it when they stand to make a greater profit," Amelia rambled on.

"There are instances, Amelia, where the law has upheld verbal commitments," Megan said, wondering if she would ever get to the bottom of the story. "Has someone failed to keep their word in some business transaction?"

"Indeed they have," came the fervent reply. "That no-good Jerome Kennedy should be run out of town."

Megan certainly agreed with that, but managed to refrain from voicing her agreement. "Just what has Mr. Kennedy done?"

"He's sold the two blocks that border the northern edge of the Bay Historical Area. The society has had their eye on that property for two years now. We were finally in a position to purchase it, only to learn that it's been sold. When we approached Jerome, and told him of our interest, he assured us he would give us first refusal. He even went so far as to waive a deposit, saying our word was good enough for him."

"Perhaps you could get in touch with the party that purchased the property, Amelia, and see if

30

you could deal with them. Do you know who bought it?"

"A large corporation by the name of Lodestar Inc.," the older woman informed her. "From what I can find out about them, they're involved in all sorts of things. I seriously doubt they would be interested in something as simple and non-profitable as a park."

"Did Jerome know that the historical society wanted the land for a park?"

"Oh, yes. And the reason we took so long in initiating the transaction was, of course, finances. We were already involved in renovating two different houses, so our means by which to purchase the land from Jerome were limited. Now we'll have to drop the whole idea, as well as hold our breaths till we see what will be built."

"I wouldn't worry too much on that last point, Amelia. That entire four-block area is restricted. That should offer you ample protection," Megan pointed out to her.

"Unfortunately the restriction ends on the south side of Spencer Street. The north side is wide open. That was the reason for our deciding to purchase the property. We'd thought to tear down those awful old buildings and have the grounds landscaped. Dogwoods, azaleas, planted along meandering, old-brick walks would have been a lovely attraction to the area."

"How did you learn of the sale?"

"My niece works in the circuit clerk's office.

31

When the transfer of title was recorded, she called me."

After assuring her elderly friend that she would do all she could to learn more about Lodestar's plans for the property, Megan cradled the receiver, then leaned back in her chair and thoughtfully stared into space.

So, as she'd suspected, Rhys Warner had merely been toying with her the evening before in his request for her to "show" him around. In order for all the legal work to have been completed and the transfer of title recorded, he would have had to bought the property weeks ago.

For the second time that morning Megan found the promise of a nice day being marred by the unwelcome encroachment of Rhys Warner into her thoughts.

There was a restlessness present in the tall, tanned man prowling about the sitting room of the motel suite that brought a speculative gleam to the eyes of the middle-aged woman sitting in one of the overstuffed chairs the room offered, a steno pad on one knee and a pencil held in readiness.

Between moments of taking dictation at a rapid pace, then long periods of silence, Stella Graham wondered just what woman had caught Rhys Warner's eye so quickly? He'd only been in Pensacola for a few days.

Stella had been his personal secretary for twelve years. She knew him as a workaholic and an indefatigable individual who expected the same from anyone around him. And yet he was scrupulously fair and paid well for the time and loyalty of his employees.

"Something troubling you, Rhys?" Stella asked softly. Only her years with him allowed her the privilege of prying. Rhys was a very private person and few people ever broke through the steel barrier he'd so carefully erected around himself. But even Stella, who worked closer with him than any of the numerous people he employed, knew better than to go beyond a certain point.

"Has Megan Colby returned my calls?" He swung around from the window and his silent study of the sweeping view of Pensacola Bay.

"No. I've called three times. Her secretary promised to give her the messages as soon as she gets to the office."

Rhys flicked back a snowy cuff with one tanned hand and glanced at the gleaming gold wristwatch. "I wasn't aware that Miss Colby kept banker's hours," he muttered in an irritated manner. "Keep trying, Stella. If you can't get her, then make an appointment for me for this afternoon."

"Are you expecting trouble from that quarter over the land you bought?"

"My business was with Jerome Kennedy. He owned something I wanted and I bought it. There was no need to involve anyone else in the transaction." He walked over and dropped to the extra long sofa, then leaned back, his hands crossed behind his dark head.

There was an air of disquiet about him, his brown eyes dark and brooding. "My business with Miss Colby . . . concerns other matters." He gave his secretary a mocking grin. "I find the lady attractive."

"I see," Stella replied without the flicker of an eyelash. "Shall I send her the usual floral offering?"

"You make flowers sound like a funeral wreath, Stella. Don't you approve?"

"No," she retorted honestly. It was a long-standing battle and one Rhys very much enjoyed. He was perfectly aware of Stella's disapproval of his life-style, and the urge to bait her was too great. He was fond of his secretary, and more than a little amused by her continued efforts to change his life.

"You know perfectly well your opinion of women is totally wrong."

"Really?"

"Of course it is," Stella told him, diving with relish into the heat of the argument. "As mundane as it may sound, there are still nice girls and bad girls, *Mr. Warner*. You, however, choose to see all women as parasites, hoping to attach themselves to a rich man."

"All but you, Stella." Rhys chuckled. "That's why you're still my favorite. Unfortunately your description is very apt."

"Well"—Stella smiled smugly—"I'm glad to see that you agree. A word of caution though. One never knows when one will find a diamond among the many imitations in life. Don't be so blinded by disillusionment that you can't recognize the real thing when you see it."

"You're a woman of firm convictions, Stella, but I'm afraid I can't buy them. There's only one thing that's important to the members of your sex, and that's money. I'm sure that's difficult for you to believe, but it's true nevertheless."

Stella stared at him and slowly shook her head. "I give up. I just hope I'm around to see you eat those words." She got up and walked over to the corner of the room where a desk and typewriter had been added to accommodate the latest guest. "Do you want me to keep those two appointments I've made to look at office space?" she crossly asked.

"I think so. With those two new shopping malls going up in Atlanta and Miami, plus the apartments here, I think Pensacola would be the most sensible location from which to operate. Once you've secured office space, call Denver and have whatever you need sent down," Rhys informed her.

Moments later, with the noise of Stella's typewriter going in the background, Rhys let his thoughts return to Megan Colby and her casual rebuff the evening before. That had intrigued and, at the same time, annoyed him. Hopefully she would prove more interesting than other women he'd known . . . for a few weeks at least. No woman held his attention for very long.

He wondered if Megan had used Jack Lindsey's

influence in obtaining her present position. Probably so, he answered his own question. There must have been considerable pressure on the board for them to have hired a woman to head up Coastal. Who better to champion her cause than the local banker?

Rhys came to a sitting position, then stood. He reached for the phone resting on a large, square table at the end of the sofa and dialed the number of the foundation.

"This is Rhys Warner," he replied to the pleasant voice that answered. "May I speak with Miss Colby please?"

"Just a moment, Mr. Warner."

There was a space of only a few seconds before Megan came on the line, her voice brisk and businesslike.

"Good morning, Mr. Warner. What can I do for you?"

For a moment Rhys was tempted to applaud her for the facade of efficiency she presented, then thought better of the idea. "I would like to drop by your office sometime today, Miss Colby, if it's convenient. There are a couple of things I'd like your opinion on."

"I'm afraid today is out of the question as far as appointments go, but what about lunch? Are you free?"

"As a matter of fact I am," he answered, a note of surprise in his voice. "Lunch will be fine. Shall I pick you up at one o'clock?"

"Thank you, but that won't be necessary. Why

don't you meet me at Apple Annie's in the Seville Quarter? Are you familiar with the location?" Megan asked. "It's on East Government Street."

"I know the place. Very well, Miss Colby, I'll see you at one."

Megan cradled the receiver, then removed her glasses and leaned back in her chair. Rhys Warner's phone call had come at the perfect moment. She'd promised Amelia to try and learn his plans for the property on Spencer Street, and what better way to pick his brain than over a nice leisurely lunch?

She'd known men like Rhys Warner before, and she wasn't about to be taken in by his charm or intimidated by his rudeness. If he really had business to discuss with her, then she'd certainly be available. If not, and he was simply using that as an excuse, she'd be equally as helpful in setting him straight—after she found out his plans for the property he'd purchased.

The remainder of the morning passed slowly, too slowly, Megan decided later, as she left the meeting with the board. There really hadn't been much of a discussion, more of a formality in deciding the issuance of industrial bonds to accommodate Corbet Industries. But, as with any meeting of that type, there were the usual grumblers and dissenters. Now Megan found herself ten minutes late for her luncheon date with Rhys Warner.

Rather than driving, she walked the few blocks

to the restaurant. She'd been unable to jog lately and needed the exercise. Although from the way the two-piece, creamy white suit with the brown camisole beneath the jacket fit her, it was evident that there was very little reason for her to worry about excess weight.

The dim passageway that led from the street past Phinias Phogg's, Rosie O'Grady's and other restaurants, and eventually to Apple Annie's at the end, was cool and inviting. As well as offering one a much-needed respite from the summer sun, it had a tendency to take one back to another era.

But today Megan resisted the urge to become lost in her historically steeped surroundings. She needed all her wits about her if she was to keep in control of her meeting with Rhys Warner.

She paused when she reached the sunlit brilliance of the open dining area, with the patio just beyond. Huge green plants lined the walls, with large hanging baskets adding their part to the tropical setting.

Behind the pinkish tint of the prescription sunglasses Megan was wearing, her blue eyes began searching the crowded space for Rhys Warner's face. It took only a moment, though, to spot him. And for a brief instant she let her soft gaze touch on the dark thrust of his head as he glanced at the menu the waiter placed before him.

Last night she'd been unable to see him clearly and she'd had to be content with conjuring up the more specific points of his features. Today, however, with the aid of her glasses his face seemed to burst into her line of vision, each feature, each line, perfectly visible. Her first impression hadn't been wrong at all, she realized as she observed the width of broad shoulders beneath the superbly cut gray suit jacket; he was huge and dangerous.

As though aware that he was being watched, Rhys chose that moment to look up, his gaze locking with Megan's hidden one. After what seemed like an immeasurable length of time, but in actuality was only a few seconds, she saw him get to his feet. At that movement from him, Megan smiled at the hostess coming toward her, then began threading her way through the tables toward the shadowed corner where Rhys awaited her.

"You're late," he told her with an indulgent caress in his voice when she joined him.

"Sorry, Mr. Warner," Megan smiled, ignoring what she read in his voice as a shy inference of habitual tardiness in women. "Hazards of my profession. Thank you," she murmured as Rhys pulled out the chair to his right and seated her.

"Surely your job isn't that demanding?" He smiled as he sat back down, his dark eyes seeming to renew its brief acquaintance with each feature of her face and every inch of her that he could see.

Don't rise to the bait, Megan, she silently lectured herself. *He's nothing but a man—more attractive than most—but a man nevertheless.* "I'm afraid so. I had a meeting at eleven o'clock that shouldn't have taken more than an hour and a half. Unfortunately, there were some people present who were determined to have their say."

The waiter appeared at that moment and Rhys looked questioningly at Megan. "Would you care for a drink?" To her request for a glass of white wine, he added another scotch and water. After the waiter had gone, Rhys once again turned his attention back to his beautiful luncheon companion. "I think the first thing we should clear up is to dismiss the Miss Colby–Mr. Warner business. My name is Rhys. May I call you Megan?"

"Please do." Megan smiled. "Remember, you're in the panhandle section of Florida. We tend to cling more to the customs of the Old South, including friendliness, than our more celebrated neighbors to the south."

"So, you obviously incorporate southern hospitality into your efforts to attract industry to this area as well as pointing out the business potential."

"I try."

"I was surprised when Jack Lindsey told me you headed up the Industrial Development Foundation. What made you choose that particular career?"

"Do I detect a note of censure in your voice?" she asked lightly, watching the play of emotions that came and went in his eyes with the rapidity of an automatic slide projector.

"Not at all. I admire a person who goes after

what they want." He slightly tipped his head forward. "Being a hard-core businesswoman, though, doesn't fit the fragile image you present."

"Then you should congratulate me on my chameleonlike ability," Megan retorted with amusement. "In answer to your question as to why I chose such a male-oriented field, the reason is simple. As a child I was a notorious tomboy. I was also raised by my dad and four older brothers. So you could say that with my rather unusual childhood, I grew up looking at the world from both a man's and a woman's point of view."

"Have you ever regretted your decision?" Rhys asked interestedly as he leaned back in his chair, one elbow propped on the arm, long tanned fingers braced beneath his stubborn chin.

"Occasionally . . . when I'm forced to deal with certain individuals who are determined to put me down, so to speak, because I am a woman. During those irrational moments I usually consider chucking it all to become antiestablishment and spend my remaining days in a commune." Suddenly she frowned. "But we don't have much of that sort of thing left, do we? Oh, well, suffice it to say that I'm human enough to want to hear a few words of praise for a job well done."

Their drinks were placed before them, and the waiter asked if they were ready to order. Megan chose the seafood crepe, while Rhys opted for the creole dish of red beans and rice with sausage and ham.

After that was dispensed with, Megan decided it was as good a time as any to broach the subject of the property he'd recently purchased. She took a sip of her wine, then met the enigmatic gaze of Rhys Warner.

"When you called this morning, you said you wanted my opinion on a couple of things. Do they concern the property you recently purchased on Spencer Street?" she asked. *Darn!* she was thinking privately. *Sitting next to him is like being subjected to a microscopic examination. I bet he'll know the exact number of hairs on my head by the time lunch is over.*

Having the full blast of his attention did little to soothe the clamor of her heart. Obviously this was a man accustomed to getting his way with women, and probably enjoyed watching them make fools of themselves in the process.

"So, my secret is out." Rhys smiled. "Is that the reason you suggested we have lunch? So that you could learn what I'm up to?"

"Of course," Megan responded without thinking, then had the grace to blush as she heard the deep chuckle rumbling deep in his chest. "I'm sorry," she offered somewhat chagrined, "that was impolite. Actually, Amelia Wrafton, who's president of the Bay Historical Society, called me earlier this morning, terribly upset. She'd just learned of the sale. The society had been promised the property by Jerome Kennedy. He even waived their offer of a deposit, assuring them that he wouldn't sell until they were financially able to buy it."

"I see," Rhys mused softly. "I assure you, Kennedy never once mentioned that fact to me. Exactly what was the society planning to do with the property? I certainly don't recall either of the two buildings being worthy of the Historical Register."

"I believe Amelia mentioned a park, complete with dogwoods, azaleas, and winding paths. As I'm sure you know, there are four blocks that make up that particular section. Unfortunately for them, the line seems to have been drawn directly down the middle of Spencer Street." Megan grimaced. "I'm sure Jerome Kennedy had his fat little finger in that maneuver as well."

"I take it you aren't on the friendliest of terms with Kennedy?"

"Let's just say he wasn't exactly thrilled by my getting the position with Coastal. His son, Tom, was the previous head of the foundation. But I don't want to bore you with that story. What I would like to know, though, strictly as a friend of the Historical Society and as an interested citizen," she hastened to clarify, "is what your plans are for the property."

"Fair enough." Rhys grinned. "But only on one condition."

"That is?"

"You take off your sunglasses. I don't like looking into two dark lenses when I'm having a conversation with a beautiful woman." He sat perfectly still, his gaze never leaving her face.

Megan felt somewhat foolish at the simple request, although she, too, found that same thing annoying when talking with someone. Deep down, however, she wasn't so sure they shared the same reasoning. Surely Rhys hadn't reached his level of success by having sunglasses banned in his presence.

With a hand that trembled slightly, she reached up and removed the offending frames from her face. Immediately the shape and size of the man sitting to her left, as well as her surroundings, became fuzzy. "I wasn't hiding, I assure you," she softly said.

Rhys studied the deep blue of her eyes and the thick fringe of lashes beneath the feathery arch of her brows with an intentness of a connoisseur about to pass judgment on some work of art. He liked what he saw and reached out and stilled her hand when she started to put the glasses back on.

"Don't," he quietly ordered her. "The view is much nicer the way it is now." His deep voice and his touch sent shivers along her spine.

Resist, Megan, resist! Her excited inner voice of caution was jumping up and down. *Let him caress someone else with his velvety eyes—you're not in his league.* With all the appearances of being calm and collected, she smiled, then said, "While I'm appreciative of the compliment—what woman wouldn't be?—and I certainly wouldn't dream of disturbing your view, Rhys, I would like to point out one small thing."

"Which is?"

"The fact that I'm practically blind without my

glasses. Minus those annoying additions to my personal wardrobe, I'd need a white cane or a dog—or both." She smiled at him. "Right now you look as though you've suddenly sprouted about three inches of fuzz."

Again he chuckled and Megan found it to be a very pleasing sound. "Then by all means put them back on," he said graciously. "I've never been likened to a caterpillar before."

Megan replaced the sunglasses, then grinned. "Presto! I promise you, you've now been returned to the perfect image of the high-powered executive."

"What about last night at dinner?" he asked, curious. "You weren't wearing glasses then."

"Jack is a close enough friend that he doesn't mind if I stumble drunkenly. He's become quite proficient at leading me around."

Lucky Jack, Rhys thought. "Wouldn't contacts help?"

"Unfortunately, no," Megan sighed. "I'm a minus twelve, a high myope. I also have superdry eyes and the contacts cause too much tearing." She reached for her glass, raised it to her lips, and took a sip of the wine. "Now that you know my secret, wouldn't you like to make me feel better by sharing some small infirmity you suffer from? Perhaps you're bald and live in fear of your hairpiece sailing through the air during a high wind?"

"No," Rhys laughed, and realized as he did so that for the first time in a long time he was intrigued by a woman rather than bored. "I promise you that if I did suffer from such a plight, I'd tell you." He leaned forward, his sudden nearness causing a tiny catch in Megan's breathing. "Have dinner with me this evening."

"I'm sorry, but I can't."

"Why not?" he asked silkily, his pleasant mood evaporating as quickly as a blanket of fog. "Does Jack Lindsey have a prior claim?"

"No," she said simply. "I won't be through at the office until seven or eight o'clock. After that many hours I wouldn't be very good company for anyone."

"May I call you later in the week?"

"Of course."

CHAPTER THREE

Megan was back in her office and at her desk when it dawned on her that Rhys Warner hadn't asked her opinion on a single thing. "While you, you goose, prattled on and on like a recording." She also hoped Amelia wouldn't call for a "progress report" as she usually referred to her follow-up calls, because Megan hadn't learned a darn thing about Rhys's plans.

She paused in her perusal of a report, remembering the warmth of his touch. Although she'd been apprehensive about seeing him, other than at the beginning of the conversation, lunch with him had been enjoyable.

More enjoyable, she reflected with wry amusement, than she really cared to admit. Even when she'd turned down his dinner invitation she'd done so with a momentary pang of regret.

Megan wasn't a babe in the woods where men were concerned. She'd always enjoyed a healthy social life and once, fleetingly, considered herself to be head over heels in love.

Being young and on her own for the first time had been exciting. During her senior year in college her dad had allowed her to have an apartment. It was as though she'd suddenly been proclaimed an adult, as well as master of her fate.

Michael Kline had seemed so perfect—kind, gentle, and thoughtful, smothering her in a cocoon of protectiveness. That kind of caring, after years of tagging along after four brothers, was mistakenly accepted by Megan as an affirmation of love. Not realizing that she wasn't the type to be content with this sort of life for very long, she willingly agreed when Michael suggested he move into her place.

It didn't take long for Megan to see that a steady diet of Michael wasn't all it was cracked up to be. She was earnestly seeking an amiable way to terminate their "arrangement" when her four brothers—in town for a university fund-raising dinner—dropped by unexpectedly to visit their "baby" sister!

The subtle hints Megan had been dropping to Michael for days, attempting to convey her unhappiness with their arrangement, took on new meaning as he stared hypnotically at the four towering Colbys, all of whom immediately sized up the situation including Michael and found him lacking.

The next morning after Megan left for class to begin taking her finals, her roommate and lover packed and left. When she returned to her small apartment for a quick lunch before going on to work at the library, she found herself once again alone.

Megan couldn't help but smile even now at how young and foolish she'd been. Nor would she ever forget her oldest brother Ian's gently spoken words that particular evening as he and the others were leaving.

"I don't like your friend, Meg. But if he suits you, then that's what counts. Remember one thing, honey. Living with a man should mean more than a few weeks or months of physical satisfaction. Think about it." He bent his dark head and kissed her warmly on the cheek. "Call me if you need anything." Then he gave her a halfhearted little grin. "Don't worry about the old man finding out, I won't tell and neither will the others."

And they didn't. But from graduation till she landed her first job in South Carolina, Megan found her brothers paying her more visits than they had during her entire college career. Nothing was ever mentioned about Michael and she was grateful. Later, she realized they had been concerned, and their impromptu visits were their way of keeping a watchful eye on her.

Occasionally, since they were in the same line of work, she and Michael would run into each other. Maturity had gone a long way toward smoothing over the embarrassing events of their initial relationship. Megan, however, had never been quite able to forget the outright panic in his face when confronted by her brothers.

"I wonder what the fearsome foursome would think of Rhys Warner?" she softly murmured. "They'd probably take to him like long-lost souls, considering they're all cut from the same cloth."

The afternoon passed with relatively few complications, with Megan finally getting to work at three thirty on her presentation for the following week. She was hoping to interest Meta Electronics enough to send someone down to look over Pensacola and the surrounding area. Meta manufactured microchips for home computers. It was the sort of high-tech industry that most members of the industrial community considered a plum.

Meta Electronics and Corbet were two entirely different types of industries, yet both were needed in a well-rounded area interested in serving all the people. Providing employment for the unskilled laborer as well as the highly trained individual added to an area's economy.

The door to her office swung open and Katie stuck her head in. "It's five o'clock, boss. Aren't you ready to call it a day?"

"I wish I could, Katie," Megan wearily remarked. She leaned back in her chair and removed her glasses, one hand gently massaging a temple. "This report's coming along nicely, but I want to go back over it and make sure I haven't left anything out."

"Can I help?" Katie asked. "I have a date with John, but it's not until eight thirty. I don't mind staying."

"Thanks, but I really need to take care of this myself. You go on and get ready for John," Megan smiled. "Just don't agree to quit your job when you marry him. Breaking in a new secretary doesn't bear thinking about."

"Don't worry," Katie reassured her. "Whoever said that two could live as cheaply as one never tried to get a veterinarian practice going."

"But just think," Megan smiled, "one day in the near future you'll look back fondly on all the scrimping and hard work."

"Do you really believe that?" Katie asked with a definite show of skepticism.

Megan shrugged. "No, but that's what I've always heard. Personally, I think people have been programmed to believe that way."

"Then when my time comes, I think I'll upset the status quo, for I'm not at all happy about having my wedding indefinitely postponed," the attractive brunette admitted.

After Katie left, Megan slipped her glasses back in place and resumed her study of the report spread out before her on the desk. In her two previous positions she'd been only one small part of a large organization. But with her present job the buck stopped with her. It was her responsibility to present the area she represented in as attractive a vein as possible.

Slowly the quietness of the building took over,

and even the sounds of the traffic on the streets faded into the background as Megan became lost in the sellable qualities of the western tip of Florida.

Time flew and it was only when the burning discomfort of cramped muscles in her neck and shoulders began to struggle for prominence in her thoughts that Megan removed her glasses, then relaxed against the high leather back of her chair.

She was exhausted and hungry, but there was also a satisfied air about her as she mentally ticked off each vital point covered in her presentation. The only thing left now was to see how great were her powers of persuasion. Her correspondence with the chairman of the board of Meta had been pleasant enough, even encouraging. But Megan was well aware that there were several other locations being considered as well.

As she became lost in thought, her shoes long since removed and forgotten, the tip of one nylon-covered foot idly touched the floor and gently swung the large chair around. While she was in Atlanta, she mused, she hoped to spend some time with her family.

Her aunt had been rather curt with Megan in her last letter, pointing out the large gap between visits. "I would suggest you find time in your busy schedule to visit your family," Beatrice Lange had written. "Otherwise your family just might feel inclined to come to you."

Megan had laughed at the not so subtle threat

and immediately called her aunt and informed her of the planned trip.

"Of course you'll be staying with us," Beatrice had assumed.

"I'm not sure, Aunt Bea. Perhaps overnight. This will be a business trip, you know," Megan tried to soothe the ruffled feelings of the older woman.

"Well, it's nice to know that you'll try to work us into your busy schedule, Megan Colby. I'm sure your father will be grateful for whatever time you choose to grant us."

Afterward Megan had called her father at his office and explained the problem.

"Don't worry, honey. Your Aunt Bea becomes unbearable if she doesn't see each of you children at least once a month. I know you're busy, and I'm proud of you. Come when you can," Francis Colby told his daughter, and Megan knew he understood. He was a surgeon and was well aware of the demands placed upon one by a career. Two of his sons had followed in his footsteps, another chose the law, and the one next to Megan was a broker with an investment firm.

The two middle boys, Edward and Timothy, were married, but Ian and Patrick were still single. Megan couldn't help but smile as she thought of the rambunctiousness of the Colby clan when they congregated at the rambling, two-story brick home in the quiet Atlanta suburb.

Yes, she thought with conviction, it was time for her to go home. She needed Aunt Bea's briskness, her brothers' outlandish teasing, and her father's gentle love.

Suddenly there was the distinct sound of the front door opening. Megan froze, panic lending its frightening edge as she caught the muffled sound of heavy footsteps coming toward her office.

With a quickness brought about by fear, she swung around in her chair to face the door, and in doing so her hand inadvertently knocked her glasses to the floor.

"It's Rhys Warner, Megan," came the deep voice from the huge shadowy figure of a man looming in the doorway.

"H—how did you get in?" she asked, unable to control the tremble in her voice.

"The door was unlocked," Rhys said as he walked toward her. "Do you usually work this late with the door wide open to anyone who wishes to drop in?"

"Of course not," Megan snapped as she slumped back in her chair, weak with relief. "It's obvious that Katie, my secretary, forgot to lock up."

"Then in the future I'd advise you to double-check the door," he suggested impatiently.

Megan endured the criticism with remarkable calm. She was so relieved that the intruder hadn't been someone intent on committing a crime, she really couldn't be angry with him.

"If you're through lecturing me, would you

please help me find my glasses?" she asked after a considerable pause had elapsed.

For a moment Rhys simply stared at her, unable to believe what he'd just heard. Damn it all! Didn't she realize that with her eyes—as blue as the sky on a summer's day—and her hair with its silky sheen, not to mention the creamy softness of her complexion, was more than enough to cause the most saintly man to have a number of less than honorable thoughts?

When an impatient movement came from Megan, Rhys stepped around the end of the desk. "Sit still," he ordered her in a terse voice. It took only a moment to locate the glasses beneath the desk. He bent down and retrieved them, then handed them to Megan.

Once the glasses were in place, she looked up at the stern features of the man towering over her and smiled. "Thank you."

"You're welcome," he scowled as he availed himself of one corner of the desk, leaning his powerful frame against it. "It's after eight. Don't you think it's time to knock off?"

"As a matter of fact I do," Megan concurred. She turned back to her desk and began neatly stacking the pages of the presentation. Several other brief adjustments were made and her desk was fairly neat and orderly. All during the time it took her to carry out these last duties, Megan was intensely aware of Rhys Warner watching her. She could almost feel his dark eyes touching every part of her, from her hair to her toes. It took considerable willpower to remain outwardly calm while withstanding the steady barrage of his gaze.

Finally she could put off the inevitable no longer. She opened the bottom desk drawer, took out her purse, then looked at her visitor. "There," she smiled. "Everything is in order and I'm through for the night."

"You're ready to go?" Rhys asked, the indentations at the corners of his mouth indicating amusement. And for the first time since he entered the room, Megan detected a distinct lessening of the coolness that had emanated so strongly from him.

"I think so," she answered somewhat hesitantly. She turned her head and looked about her, swiveling in her chair. "There's not another door to check and the light switch is over there." She nodded toward the wall next to the reception room."

Before Megan could guess his intentions, Rhys went down on his haunches close beside her chair and scooped up her shoes, dangling them before her small nose on two square-tipped fingers. "I think you'll be more comfortable with these, don't you?" he asked, his face on a level with hers.

Megan's surprised gaze swung from the taupe-colored sandals to the dancing merriment in Rhys's eyes, then downward to the sensuous curve of his mouth. His lips were only slightly parted in a teasing grin and she found herself more than a little curious as to how those lips would feel against her own.

Mercifully it was Rhys who broke the electric moment, but in a manner that threw Megan into a greater state of disquiet. With the ease of one accustomed to such practices, he set the shoes on the floor, caught one of her feet in his hand, and slipped the high-heeled sandal on, then did the same with the other.

When he'd finished he looked at Megan, noting the telltale blush that stained her cheeks. "According to the fairy tale, if the slipper fits, the prince and princess live happily ever after. I'm not sure what's supposed to happen when both slippers fit."

"In this case, Prince, I'd say you picked a dud." Megan struggled to bring the tense moment back to normal. "I remember Cinderella as a petite blond beauty, content to have her life arranged by others."

"All of which is totally unacceptable to one Megan Colby, correct?" Rhys asked seductively.

"Correct. I'm afraid I'm an opinionated, nearsighted gal whose main concern is my career."

"Even the tempting inducement of Jack Lindsey's wealth and position doesn't cause you some anxious moments?" There was an imperceptible narrowing of his hooded gaze as he waited for her answer.

"Just what makes you think I've been asked to share Jack's wealth or position?" Megan asked, amazed to find herself having this remarkable conversation with a man she'd met only the evening before and not feeling in the least embarrassed.

"Hasn't he?"

"Yes."

"Are you stringing him along until you tire of your career image? Keeping him interested by a few well-planned hints that you're considering his proposal?" For a moment Megan caught the distinct flicker of disgust mirrored in his eyes, only to see it just as quickly shuttered.

"I'm sorry to disappoint you, Rhys, but Jack is a friend. Nothing more, and he knows it. Now"— she glanced once more at her desk in an effort to calm herself—"if you don't have any other insulting accusations to charge me with, will you please move? My day started at six thirty this morning and, frankly, I'm worn out."

Rhys rose to his full height, then extended his hand to her. "I'm sorry." The apology was, without a doubt, the most ungracious one she'd ever heard.

Megan pointedly eyed him as she accepted his hand and stood. "Obviously you aren't accustomed to saying those words very often." Her voice was brisk and cool. "You should try it more often. Believe me, it won't cause your hair or your teeth to fall out, nor have I ever heard of it killing anyone."

"There's always the first time," Rhys countered silkily, his hand automatically cupping her elbow as they walked toward the door.

Megan reached for the light switch, then paused, turning her head and staring up at him. "I agree. For someone as arrogant as you, it could prove fatal." With ill-disguised grace she flipped the switch and stalked across the reception room to the outer door.

When she reached the street and turned to the parking lot at the side of the building, she felt Rhys's detaining hand on her arm. Megan stopped, then turned and faced him. "Now what?" she demanded frostily.

"Have dinner with me." There was strength in the six-foot-plus frame, not to mention enough arrogance for ten men. He exuded an air of self-confidence that was challenging. As Megan allowed her gaze to sweep over him in an attempt to pierce the wall of assurance surrounding him, she was unable to suppress the grim admiration she felt for him as a man, and for his unqualified success in business. Even the way he dressed drew her approval.

There was something about Rhys Warner that intrigued her. One minute he was charming her with words, with his eyes, and the next thing she knew he would change before her very eyes, becoming a hostile, embittered man.

"I'm not in the mood for the sort of sarcastic sparring you seem to enjoy, Rhys, especially this evening."

"Is the truth so hard to take?"

The look of grim admiration mirrored in her eyes quickly turned to disbelief as she stared at him. "I really can't decide if my hearing has gone or if you're slightly crazy!" Megan exclaimed. "Believe it or not, Rhys, I'm not asking for nor do I want your approval. And if I choose to lead every man in Florida down the garden path, I fail to see how it concerns you. In other words, Mr. Warner, I find you to be arrogant, bossy, and carrying a tremendous chip on your shoulder."

Without even a backward glance Megan left the astounded Rhys standing in the middle of the sidewalk and hurried to her car.

"Damn!" she muttered more than once beneath her breath as she unlocked her car, got in, and started the engine, then raced out of the parking lot. For a little while, before turning into some sort of crazed person, Megan had found herself drawn to the man. At lunch she'd ably parried his supposedly innocent little digs, then gone on and enjoyed his company.

His appearance at her office—aside from frightening the daylights out of her—had been looked upon as an unexpectedly pleasant way to round off a day. But all his charm and any other redeeming qualities he might possess wasn't inducement enough for her to quietly and meekly allow him to have his little moments of revenge against the entire female race at her expense.

What you're most upset about, she told herself, *is the fact that for the first time you've found a man you're really attracted to.*

"So why, by all that's holy, does he have to consider me as some sort of public enemy number one?" she muttered beneath her breath. Had he been hurt by someone in his past, Megan wondered as she drove. With his wealth and position he could probably have any woman he desired.

The mystery surrounding Rhys Warner deepened, and Megan found herself at a loss even to begin to understand. What she did feel, however, was a sudden sense of depression, which she immediately tried to ignore.

By the time she reached her apartment, her anger had cooled somewhat, but not enough to totally erase the heightened color in her cheeks.

After changing from the clothes she'd worn to work into a pair of faded navy shorts and a white halter that had seen better days, Megan padded barefoot, and minus her glasses, into her small kitchen and began to consider what she'd have for dinner.

A salad wouldn't do it, she decided as she stood in front of the open fridge. The lunch she'd had with Rhys Warner was many hours in the past and she was starving. Perhaps a steak, baked potato, and a salad, she thoughtfully mused. By using the microwave to defrost the steak, then bake the potato, her dinner wouldn't be longer than a few minutes to prepare.

Without pausing to change her mind, Megan reached for the handle to the freezer compartment just as her doorbell sounded. "Who can that be?" she frowned, then shrugged. Probably Jack, she thought as she walked unhurriedly through the living room. He sometimes dropped by unexpectedly.

There was a friendly grin on her face as she opened the door. "Can't find anyone to—" But Rhys Warner, not Jack, was propped against the doorjamb, one hand tucked finger-deep in the front pocket of his slacks, the other arm holding a large brown bag, the white-paper-wrapped end of a loaf of French bread sticking out.

The look of shock on Megan's face at learning the identity of her caller didn't go unnoticed by Rhys. Nor did the brevity of the shorts and halter she was wearing.

Had Megan been wearing her glasses, she would have seen the subtle narrowing of brown eyes as they lingered on the gentle swell of her breasts and the slim, tanned length of her legs. A peculiar glint surfaced in the course of his brief scrutiny, one that would have had Megan inordinately curious, had she seen it.

"I've come to apologize, Megan," he said, his voice deep and warm. "May I come in? I've brought our dinner," he added on a teasing note.

Suddenly the depression that had hovered over her earlier was lifted, and Megan found herself as light-headed as a teenager.

"Only if you promise to leave your nasty remarks outside," she smiled as she stepped back and waved him in.

"I promise," Rhys said, stepping into the room. But instead of simply walking by her, Megan saw him stop and turn toward her. Before she knew it, she felt the warm softness of his lips pressed against hers and the fingers of one large hand splayed over her back.

After the first startling seconds Megan drew back, embarrassed to find herself breathless. "Does . . . does that go along with *all* your apologies?" she murmured, the color in her cheeks heightened by pleasure and confusion.

Rhys smiled down at her, some inexplicable something stirring in his ice-laden heart as he watched the telltale signs in her face. "You have my word, Megan, that it's a first. And if I suddenly become toothless and bald, I'm holding you personally responsible. Apologies usually aren't given a second thought by me, but in this particular instance I'm finding the practice extremely enjoyable."

"My, my," she sighed, smiling at the delightful upswing in her evening. "After all that, what can a poor girl do?"

"Show me the way to your kitchen, please, before I'm forced to start eating this paper bag. I'm starving," he shot back.

"Men," she snorted in feigned disgust as she turned and led the way to the kitchen. "Whatever happened to all those knights in shining armor I was told about as a little girl?"

"They probably starved to death waiting for the fair maidens to make up their minds," Rhys retorted blandly. He placed the bag on the butcher block and began removing the groceries.

It was Megan, staring intently at his purchases,

her eyes screwed up in a definite squint, that brought an amused chuckle from Rhys. "Go get your glasses, Megan, and put them on. You look like an angry chipmunk glaring at me."

"Gee," she drawled interestedly. "Earlier I was cast as a designing female with questionable intent. Now I'm likened to a small furry creature." She looked thoughtfully at him for several seconds. "I wonder which of us it is that can't make up their minds?"

CHAPTER FOUR

When Megan returned to the kitchen some five minutes later, having not only added her glasses but a shirt as well, she found the small, compact space to be a veritable beehive of activity.

In the short time she'd been out of the room, Rhys had divested himself of his jacket and tie. The collar of his white shirt was open, the sleeves turned back over tanned forearms covered by a dark sprinkling of fine hair.

In addition to the changes in his dress, he'd also popped two thick, succulent steaks on the grill section of the air-jet stove. Two large Idahos were likewise baking in the microwave, and Rhys was calmly assembling the ingredients for a salad.

"Please, tell me that your services as a chef are for hire and I'll keep you booked for at least three evenings a week," Megan told him, twitching her nose appreciatively at the aroma permeating the room. She paused beside him and filched a rib of celery.

"I suppose I could arrange something." He looked up from his work and grinned. "For a price, of course."

"Of course." Megan shrewdly eyed him before turning and reaching into one of the cupboards for the plates. "For a moment I almost forgot that nasty little habit you have of equating everything and everyone in terms of dollars and cents."

"My image—you understand." Rhys remained unperturbed as he continued to chop and tear his way through a bowlful of vegetables. "If you've done any checking on me"—he flashed her a knowing look, then went on with his chore—"you must have read that I'm what is commonly referred to as a self-made man. So you'll forgive, I hope, any rough edges that might surface from time to time. Being poor left its mark on me."

"Which is merely an excuse for your rude and arrogant behavior," Megan bluntly retaliated. She carried the tray holding the plates, glasses, napkins, and cutlery to the table, and began arranging the two place settings. "Any rough edges you might have would certainly be labeled self-made. They're conjured up in your mean little brain just to throw people off stride—place them at a disadvantage."

"Hmmm . . ." Rhys mused as he added salt and fresh ground pepper to the salad. "That line al-

66

ways worked for me before; why doesn't it have any effect on you?"

"Quite possibly because I grew up listening to my chauvinistic brothers as they sought to undermine the core of femininity with their equally disgusting stories. So your poor-boy routine can be reserved for someone else; I'm not impressed. Poverty doesn't automatically negate common courtesy," she told him with brutal certainty.

Privately, Rhys was amused by her blatantly thumbing her nose at him. His first estimation of her as having used Jack Lindsey's influence in gaining her present position seemed to be totally misleading. But, then, weren't all women born with that incredible ability to appear as innocent as the driven snow? Hadn't he learned, to his regret, that talk was cheap and that promises became meaningless when a woman was faced with a choice of remaining true to her commitments or discarding her old love without a second glance and latching on to what she considered a better catch?

The food was delicious and Megan wasted no time in telling Rhys so. She wasn't at all embarrassed to find that he was as good a cook as she, and apprised him of that fact when he pointed out that some women might resent his capabilities in the kitchen.

"That's ridiculous," she scoffed. "I for one think life's too short to worry about who's more talented in certain areas than others. So"—she flashed him a mischievous grin over the rim of her wineglass—"anytime anyone—male or female—wishes to prepare me a delicious meal, I'll graciously accept and praise their efforts to the skies." A thoughtful expression slowly replaced the cheerful one. "Were you hoping I'd feel some discomfort or anxiety by you flaunting your culinary skills?"

"Certainly not." Rhys laughed. "I did expect a certain amount of praise though, which you gave." He leaned back, his expression unfathomable. "What I really wanted was to have dinner with you."

"Which you have had," Megan softly reminded him, quietly enduring his thorough survey of her features.

"As you say." His dark head tipped forward fractionally. "But I'm still puzzled by you, Megan."

"Oh?"

"If Jack Lindsey is only a friend, is there some other man in your life?"

"No."

"Have you ever been married?"

"No," Megan smiled. "Now it's my turn, counselor. Are you married, divorced, engaged, presently living with, or contemplating any of the aforementioned arrangements?" she asked, looking him straight in the eye as the words tumbled from her lips.

Even though her question was asked under the guise of friendly teasing, underneath it all lay an inexplicable urge to know more about Rhys

Warner than the flattering account revealed in the personal profiles she'd found in a manufacturer's weekly manual earlier in the day.

"I was divorced years ago," he revealed without hesitation. "I'm single, with no encumbrances at the present. Okay?"

The two words that stood out in Megan's mind were divorce and encumbrance. Was this woman he'd been married to so long ago the reason behind the less than flattering opinion that surfaced from time to time when he spoke of the opposite sex?

There was a curious flash of resentment in Megan that he'd include her in his blanket contempt for women in general.

"Does the idea that I'm divorced bother you?" Rhys broke the sudden silence that hovered over them. There was a cynical lilt in his voice and in the burnished glow of his eyes that raked her with disbelief.

Megan met his look with her own charged one. "Other than the momentary sense of regret that one normally feels, no. I do, however, resent your careless or deliberate—I'm not sure which—reference to women as encumbrances. Just what makes you an authority on the subject?" As her temper grew, so did the rash of words that spilled from her lips. "If, and I repeat, if you were wronged or unfairly used by your former wife, then what's the big deal? You've obviously refused to let her memory hamper your climb to the top in the financial world. What baffles me is why, with your intelligence, you have decided that every woman you meet must be looked upon as a second-rate citizen because of one lousy curve fate chose to throw you."

"And just what do you base your rash assumptions on, Miss Colby?" Rhys spoke icily into the electrified silence that followed her outburst.

"Why, it's evident in the way you speak, the expression that comes and goes in your eyes when you feel the urge to twist the knife a little deeper in the back of the whole of womanhood."

"Womanhood?" he sneered. "My God! You sound like some damn suffragette screaming and carrying on about women's rights. Problem is," he continued on in the same brutal voice, "you don't know what the hell you're talking about. You're so damned wrapped up in proving to the world that you can function and compete equally as well, and, in some cases, better than a man, that you've become an instant authority on everything from fertilizer to the atom bomb!"

"In that case, Mr. Warner, I'm sure it won't come as a surprise when I ask you to leave," Megan snapped, her anger in full force and only barely held in check. How dare he sit at her table, in her very own apartment and hurl such degrading insults at her!

"Oh, no." Rhys got to his feet, then walked over to an antique tea cart standing in one corner of the small dining area. "You opened this can of worms, so don't you think you should see it through?" He poured a generous portion of scotch into a glass, added two ice cubes and a whisper of water, then turned back around and faced his glaring hostess.

"Contrary to your fanciful flights of imagination, my dear, I divorced my wife because I couldn't live with a woman who deliberately aborted a normal, healthy pregnancy and was also a hopeless alcoholic. Another of her cute little tricks was that she didn't care where or with whom she spent the night. Three years after our divorce she was killed in a car wreck. She and her boyfriend were drunk at the time."

He picked up the drink as well as the bottle of scotch and returned to his chair opposite Megan.

"I—I'm sorry," she murmured, thinking how horrible it must have been for him to have lost his unborn child, as well as watch someone he loved destroy herself.

"Don't waste your pity on me or Alexis, Megan," Rhys murmured cruelly. "It was my money that interested her, and her beauty that intrigued me until we both tired of the charade. My personal moment of pleasure on learning of the pregnancy was the only decent thing to come of our union." He raised the glass to his lips and drained half the mixture in one gulp, his cold gaze never leaving Megan's shocked face.

"But surely, I mean, there had to be some sort of love at the beginning. I can't believe two sane people would marry for such meaningless reasons?" She protested the cold, calculating picture he'd painted. She continued to stare at him, catching a glimpse of the tortured soul of Rhys Warner and was shocked to the core at what that brief moment revealed.

"Love?" He smiled scornfully. "Ah, yes, for a moment I'd forgotten. You think all marriages are made in heaven, don't you? You grew up surrounded by love." He slowly shook his head. "Love is something I stopped believing in along with Santa Claus when I was four years old."

"W-were you poor as a child?" she asked hesitantly. Dear God! she thought wildly, she had indeed opened a can of worms. And even though what she'd learned was far from pretty, she wanted to hear anything he would tell her. There was something about Rhys that was equally fascinating and frightening.

Her avid curiosity where Rhys was concerned reminded her of when she was a child, armed with all sorts of parental admonishments not to go near or do a certain thing for fear of getting hurt. But childlike, that streak of rebellion surfaced and momentarily overtook her and propelled her to uncover Rhys's secrets.

"All children raised in orphanages are poor." He shrugged. "But at least everyone is the same. Actually, it wasn't so bad. You couldn't miss what you'd never had. We had three meals a day and clothes on our backs."

"Were . . . are your parents dead?" Megan stammered over the question.

"Nothing so kind, I assure you. My father deserted his family when I was three. Rather than take on the responsibility of raising her son by herself, my mother put me in the orphanage." There was a significant arching of one heavy, dark brow as he spoke. "Needless to say, we're not very close."

"No . . ." Megan softly murmured. "I can see that you wouldn't be." Then she lapsed into a pensive silence.

Was it too late to teach this strangely brooding man about love and trust between two people? Did she even dare to try? But Megan knew the answers even before she asked the questions. She'd never met a man who had disturbed her thoughts like Rhys had. She was irresistibly drawn to him, and she had a feeling that only time and patience would allow her a glimpse of the man beneath the hurt, disappointment, and bitterness that had been building in him for years.

With a tremulous smile softening her lips, Megan eased back her chair and stood. "You finish your drink while I take care of the dishes."

As she moved about the kitchen, Rhys seemed to recover from his dark mood and began questioning her about the different projects she was working on, becoming unusually interested when she mentioned the electronics firm and the upcoming trip.

"I only hope I can generate enough interest to get them to add Pensacola to the list of perspective sites they'll be considering in the coming months. I definitely know of two other locations in competition with us and naturally"—she threw

Rhys, who was sprawled in his chair, one hand clasping the glass that held his scotch, a pert grin —"I think we have more to offer."

She closed the dishwasher, wiped off the counter, then looked at her guest. "Would you like some coffee or more scotch?"

"I'll stick with the scotch, unless it bothers you." Rhys lost no time in stating his preference.

"Hardly," Megan assured him. "With a father and four brothers, I'm not likely to fall apart over a few drinks of an alcoholic beverage."

With their appetites sated, they deserted the hard chairs at the table for the more comfortable cushions of the living room sofa. The wine, the excellent food, plus an exciting man to share them with, had lulled Megan into a state of lazy contentment. Even the explosive outburst between them earlier seemed to have had a strange cathartic effect upon this new and fragile relationship developing between them.

But her very pleasant state of affairs became charged with the subtle undercurrents of tension when Rhys reached for her hand, his grasp warm and firm, and suddenly she was aware of every single aspect of the man beside her.

"Have you made reservations for the Atlanta trip?" he asked, turning so that he was almost facing her, letting his other arm settle on the back of the sofa behind her shoulders.

Megan inhaled shakily, feeling slightly giddy as she bore the brunt of the full force of his attention. She gave him the name of the hotel, then added, "I'm planning on staying only one night. Hopefully, I'll spend whatever time is left with my dad."

"Still playing at being the dutiful daughter?" he taunted her in a soft voice.

Megan refused to take exception to the remark. She merely gave him a considering look and shrugged. "I don't pretend to enjoy being with my father or anyone else, Rhys. I'm long past the age where I find it necessary to resort to such childish games."

Even as she spoke she felt the whispery caress of his thumb against the wildly beating pulse at her wrist.

"The calm exterior you're trying so hard to present seems at odds with what your heart's telling me," he pointed out with maddening accuracy, the arm behind her slipping effortlessly to her shoulders where the fingers of that hand began to softly knead the taut muscles of her neck and shoulders.

"So," she smiled gently. "I'm somewhat of a fraud. I . . . find it extremely, er, exciting to be entertaining such a . . . a distinguished gentleman." She delicately arched her brows at the last two words.

The barely audible rumble of laughter deep in his chest was the first honest indication she'd had all evening that he was relaxed. With this startling realization came a slow, steady warmth that spread itself over her entire body.

"If the distinguished gentleman were to ask the

sassy lady for a kiss, do you think she would turn into an outraged defender of women's rights or would she become the warm, passionate woman I think exists behind that façade of professionalism?"

The silence was deafening. Megan could almost imagine she could actually hear her own eyes blinking. There were questions jumping and leaping in both their gazes that were irrevocably locked in the moment of decision. She wondered fleetingly what would happen if she said no to this complex man who had entered her life so suddenly. Would he persist in allowing that innate feminine characteristic of wanting to be pursued while at the same time disclaiming any knowledge of the chase to erupt?

But as soon as the question was posed, Megan knew the answer. Rhys wasn't the type of man to indulge in the frivolous machinations of some woman's idea of her supreme right to be indulged by a man.

No, she reasoned in that heightened moment, *if I behave like an emptyheaded fool, I'll probably never see him again.* And she knew with uncanny insight that telling Rhys no was the furthest thing from her mind.

"If the decision is such a difficult one," he gruffly broke into the frantic workings of her mind. "Then perhaps I should have acted rather than asked." All the while he was speaking, his arm about her shoulders was drawing her to him.

His other hand released hers to snake out and fit itself to the curve of her waist.

Just before the soft glow from the table lamp at one end of the sofa was blocked out by the shape of his head, Megan caught the sparkling highlights that danced amid the thick darkness of his hair.

Then in a simultaneous move, or so it seemed to her, she felt her glasses being eased from her face and the warmth of Rhys's lips covering hers. The exchange had occurred so swiftly, so effortlessly, that before she had time to miss the first, she was feeling the second.

The unexpected gentleness of the kiss momentarily stunned Megan. She'd tried to imagine how his lips would feel, but imagination and the real thing were light-years apart. Any futile notions of resistance she might have entertained were swept away as she responded to the urgency of the demands he was seeking from her.

When it seemed that the total dominance of her lips weren't enough, Rhys shifted both their bodies around so that Megan found herself half lying across his hard thighs, her breasts pressed against the thickness of his chest.

Without conscious thought she slowly inched her arms upward to encircle the strong column of his neck, drawing her body into even closer contact with his. There was a rough sigh of satisfaction from Rhys as if he had interpreted her meaning, absorbed it and was now intent on leading her through yet another maze of passion, a passion which had been ignited by him, and was being fanned and fed by the sweeping warmth of his hands as they moved over her.

But it was the warm insinuation of his large hand through the opening of her blouse and beneath the now gaping cup of the halter she wore beneath, that jolted Megan from the world of passion and desire nipping at her.

She stiffened as the thrust of Rhys's thumb grazed the rigid tip of her breast, his palm cupping and holding the creamy mound.

Megan pulled on every ounce of self-control she possessed to draw herself back from the edge of an abyss of pleasure that beckoned her into its swirling midst of sensual awakening. Rhys sensed the abrupt swing in her emotions and slowly withdrew his hand.

She opened her eyes and, though his features were blurred, nothing could hide the outline of the face she'd committed to memory. Megan raised a hand and let the tips of her fingers rest against the stubborn thrust of his chin.

"Please, Rhys, I—"

"Don't say it," he murmured huskily, catching her hand and pressing his lips against the palm. There was a hint of resignation in his voice, and Megan could barely make out the ghost of a smile touching his lips. "Now that I have the answer to that question I asked earlier, Megan Colby, I plan to become a very visible part of your future."

"Don't I have any say in the matter?" she asked with feigned haughtiness. Having tasted a sampling of him as a lover, and knowing how readily she'd responded left her in the unenviable position of hoping to strike a happy, if not face-saving, medium by attempting to inject an air of humor into the startling situation.

"No discussion," Rhys answered, burying his fingers in the softness of her hair and slowly withdrawing them, seeming fascinated with the way the dark tendrils clung to his skin.

"The strong, silent type, huh?" Megan grinned, finding the verbal exchange to be equally as fascinating as his lovemaking.

"Please, remember that I'm a poor working girl, and unaccustomed to the worldly ways of a real live tycoon." She gave him her laziest southern drawl, adding the exaggerated fluttering of her thick lashes.

"As much as I hate to interrupt your outstanding performance as a vamp," he smiled, "don't you think you could do a better job of it if you could see me?" Before Megan could reply, he leaned forward and swooped up her glasses, then settled them in place on her face.

She quickly adjusted the fit, favoring him with a harsh glare as she did so. "A gentleman would never dare refer to the fact that the lady in his arms is blind as a post."

"Tsk, tsk." Rhys laughed as he dropped a light kiss on her forehead. "I'm no gentleman, and your vanity is unbelievable. It's very difficult to keep a straight face with you scowling at me like a tiny barn owl."

With an injured toss of her head and a loud sniff, Megan pushed herself from his lap, not stopping till she was pressing against the over-stuffed arm of the sofa. "Good night, Mr. Warner. You're marvelous in the kitchen, but as a conversationalist, you stink!"

"You left out your assessment of me as a lover, Megan," he tacked on silkily. "Do you think the appetizer was palatable enough to cause you to want to sample the main course?"

For a moment Megan was tempted to lash out with some scathing cut-down, but thought better of the idea. She would look rather silly raising ridiculous objections to something they both knew she'd enjoyed as much as he had.

And yet it didn't take a genius to see that Rhys was accustomed to moving ahead—be it business or women—at a far greater speed than Megan. The question left her floundering. She wanted to see more of him, but if she did, she knew it would lead to a serious reckoning. He wouldn't be as easily managed as the Michael Klines of her life or even Jack Lindsey. Was she ready for the sort of upheaval Rhys would surely bring into her life?

She turned her head and found him watching her. "Do you always take so long making up your mind, Megan?" And for the first time there was kindness in his smile.

"No, not usually," she honestly admitted. "But, then, I've never met a man quite like you." She felt herself weakening beneath his watchful eye. "There's something about you that causes

80

me to stop and weigh each word, each gesture." She dropped her eyes in embarrassment. "Sounds silly, doesn't it?"

Suddenly she felt the cushion she was sitting on give, caught the faint spicy smell of shaving lotion, and raised her head as a large, capable hand slid beneath her chin. "Not silly at all— more cautious, I'd say. An emotion I can understand much easier than the usual coyness that seems to come so effortlessly from some women. I'm finding you to be a painfully honest female, Megan. Something I'd begun to think extinct."

"You make me sound like a *National Geographic* special," she frowned.

"Special, yes," he said gruffly. "You're also hot-tempered, beautiful, and a bit of a flirt. And," he rasped in a near whisper, "we're good together."

Megan felt her body slipping beneath the spell of his dark, gleaming eyes and the seductive timbre of his voice. Her senses were welded together in one single point of awareness as his thumb traced the sensuous curve of her lips, lips that only moments before had yielded so willingly to him in a storm of awareness that had shocked her.

"Will you have dinner with me tomorrow evening?" he whispered against one corner of her mouth, his lips following the trail left by the soothing brush of his thumb.

"Yes." The word flowed toward him on a sigh of pleasure, and then his mouth took possession of her trembling one. When his arms caught her to him, Megan closed her mind to all but the darting prisms of excitement bursting within her.

Surely this infatuation was just that, and would pass after a few dates. Wouldn't it? Of course, she dreamily concurred as her fingers sought the rough springiness of Rhys's dark hair. He was exciting, sexy as sin, and his presence would be an attractive addition to what remained of the summer months.

CHAPTER FIVE

Megan awoke on Saturday morning with a sense of well-being that it was the weekend and that for two whole days she needn't worry about charts, graphs, or the state of the economy in her particular corner of the world.

She stretched her slim, sleep-warmed body and yawned hugely, then settled back to let her thoughts linger on Rhys. It had been over a week now since she'd first met him for lunch at Apple Annie's in the Seville Quarter. Since that time, hardly an evening had gone by that they hadn't seen each other.

Dinner with him the evening before, then quiet conversation afterward over delicious cups of Irish coffee reminded her again that he wasn't one of those men who dominated the conversation with wild excerpts from his past. Instead, he gently urged Megan to talk about herself.

He seemed inordinately curious about her family, and asked endless questions about her brothers.

Later, as they were dancing, it suddenly occurred to her that she'd done most of the talking, answered all the questions Rhys had put to her, without him actually revealing anything more about himself than she'd learned that first evening at her apartment.

This realization brought a thoughtful quietness to Megan that had Rhys watching her consideringly. When he took her home, neither seemed in the mood for further conversation. In fact, the kiss he gave her at her door could almost have been called an afterthought in that he appeared to be as wrapped up in his own thoughts as she was in hers.

When he left her there'd been no mention of their seeing each other over the weekend.

Megan wondered, fleetingly, if she'd given him the impression that she'd sit patiently by the phone waiting for him to call. Or could it be that he already had plans?

Neither of the conclusions sat well with her, and in a matter of seconds her attractive face wore a frown as she considered the possibility that Rhys hadn't been deep in thought at all, but bored stiff!

"Perhaps we don't go together as well as he first thought," she muttered darkly. *Stop being ridiculous!* Her conscience put an immediate stop to her runaway thoughts. *Be thankful he didn't come in or you quite probably would have wound up in bed with him!*

Megan's mouth pulled ruefully to one side as she silently acknowledged the truth of her fruitful imaginations.

Rhys traveled in the fast lane of life, and deep down she was forced to admit that she was no match for him. He was cynical and brittle, and Megan, who'd been fortunate to enjoy a life surrounded by people who loved and encouraged her, found herself experiencing tiny pangs of guilt.

"Which is not a very sensible approach," she muttered as she threw back the covers and swung her feet to the floor. "I'm not about to shoulder a guilt trip simply because I was more fortunate than he." But as she spoke she knew instinctively that Rhys wasn't the sort of man to want pity from anyone, especially from a woman.

He was a complex person and Megan hadn't the slightest idea how to deal with him—if indeed she was given the chance. Nor could she honestly say she didn't want to see him again.

The morning inched along at a snail's pace as she gave her apartment a quick going-over, then made a shopping list. With the upcoming trip to Atlanta, the visit to the supermarket would be a quick one.

Just as she jotted down the last item, the phone sounded shrill and harsh in the quietness of the apartment. With a quickness that betrayed the sense of disquiet hovering in the back of her mind all morning, Megan reached for the receiver of the wall phone by the counter and held it to her ear.

"Hello?"

"Hi, Megan," came Jack Lindsey's cheerful voice. "What's going on?"

"Need you ask that question of a working girl on a Saturday morning?" she responded brightly, masking the disappointment she felt when it wasn't Rhys. "Don't you men have to spend any time at all performing such mundane chores as cleaning and shopping?"

"Believe me," Jack laughed, "I try very hard not to. Will you be through by this evening?"

"As far as I know. Why?"

"There's a party over at the Summerses. Would you like to go?"

"Sounds nice," said Megan. "What time?"

"Around eight, and the dress is casual."

They chatted on for a few more minutes and, when Megan cradled the receiver, a sigh of disappointment eased unnoticed past her lips, disappointment that it hadn't been Rhys Warner asking her out rather than Jack. But sitting at home and waiting for a man to call simply wasn't her style, regardless of how attractive she found him to be.

By the time she returned from her shopping trip, Megan had talked herself into a better frame of mind. After all, she reasoned, Jack was always fun to be with. She'd even managed to work up some enthusiasm for the evening ahead.

As soon as she put away her groceries, she went to her bedroom and over to the closet, where she began looking over what she had in the way of something casual to wear. Leigh Summers might very well say casual, but from experience Megan knew her hostess would be dressed to the teeth.

She finally settled on a jumpsuit of fine Indian voile, with tiny hand-painted pink roses and minute flecks of gold scattered over the soft blue background. The bodice consisted of a criss-crossed neckline, and was sleeveless. Extravagantly full legs fell from a fitted waist, with narrow elasticized cuffs at the ankles.

She carried the jumpsuit over to the bed and laid it down and was in the process of taking down high-heeled sandals, when the phone sounded. Again her heart quickened as she turned and hurried to answer.

This time, however, there was no cause for disappointment, for it was Rhys.

"You sound out of breath," he said huskily as Megan gripped the receiver and sank to the edge of the bed.

"No," she tried for a less revealing tone of voice. "I was looking for something in the closet." Then she thought how ridiculous that sounded. A fool could tell she was excited.

"Did you find it? Whatever it was you were looking for?"

"Yes. I'm afraid it was nothing more fascinating than a pair of shoes," she explained.

"Getting ready for your trip already?" Rhys asked.

"Not exactly," Megan carefully evaded the question. "Are you calling from your office?" she asked in an attempt to change the subject.

"As a matter of fact I am. My secretary finally decided on a place for us and we've somewhat moved in." He named one of the newer executive complexes not far from Megan's office. "Knowing Stella as I do, I'm sure she'll have everything well organized by Monday morning."

"She sounds very efficient," Megan said pleasantly. "Won't she mind giving up her weekend though?" She had no difficulty at all conjuring up an image of the sort of individual he'd have as a secretary.

"Stella is in her early fifties, Megan, and has been with me for over twelve years." Rhys offered that bit of information unhesitatingly.

"Oh . . . I see."

"Good," he smoothly countered. "Now there won't be any question in your mind as to whether or not I sleep with my secretary, will there?"

"To be honest, I'd only gotten as far as picturing her as some curvaceous something or other. My fertile imagination hadn't quite gotten the two of you in bed," she admitted, and was rewarded for her honesty by the sound of Rhys's deep laughter filling her ear.

"Have dinner with me this evening."

"I'm sorry, Rhys," Megan answered in a flat voice. "But I can't."

"Surely you aren't working over the weekend?"

"No, I'm not working." Her tone was short. "I have a date." Did he think all she had to fill her life was her career? That men in general found her unattractive?

"Who's the lucky guy?" The coolness of his question was not lost on Megan.

"Jack Lindsey. We're going to a party at a friend's house," she replied.

"In that case I won't keep you. Have fun." Before she could utter a single word, Megan heard the sharp click of the receiver being dropped in place, then the steady buzzing of the dial tone.

She sat staring in stunned surprise for a few minutes, then slowly replaced the receiver. Not only did Rhys have a black outlook where women were concerned, his manners left a great deal to be desired.

Later that evening, as Megan dressed, she found her anger toward Rhys had slowly faded and in its stead was a peculiar sense of regret. She remembered the evening at her office and the disappointment she'd felt after their harsh exchange, and then how relieved she'd been when she opened the door to him a short time later.

In the course of her adult life Megan had heard the phrase "love at first sight," and had often scoffed at such a thing existing. But she always thought back to her own parents, who had known each other for only three short weeks before they married.

"But loving Rhys and finding him attractive are two entirely different things," she murmured as she applied a pale violet shade of eye shadow to her lids. "I seriously doubt he'll ever let any woman get close enough to really know him, much less love him."

The Summers's home was ultra-modern in design, with huge expanses of glass in each room as well as cathedral ceilings. The decor bore the same modernistic influence. This second visit to the house left Megan with the same impression as the first; she felt she'd stumbled upon a prototype for homes for the year two thousand.

To her, the only two redeeming qualities regarding the structure were the large patio between the pool and the glass doors leading from the enormous den. The other was, that without her glasses, the sterile glass and chrome was seen through a gentle haze.

It was on the patio that the sumptuous buffet and bar were set up, with individual tables capable of accommodating one or two couples scattered around the pool.

After their arrival Jack immediately whisked two drinks from the tray of a passing waiter. He handed one to Megan and kept the other for himself. They lingered for a few minutes and chatted with Leigh Summers, then moved on and joined a noisy group that included mutual friends. By the time Jack eventually steered Megan toward the buffet, she was having no difficulty remembering that breakfast had been her last meal.

"Some bash, huh?" he spoke close to her ear in order to be heard over the music coming from the built-in speakers on the patio.

"I'll say. They really know how to spend Daddy's money, don't they?" she quipped as they heaped their plates. "You'll have to tell me what half this food is, because I can't make it all out."

"You'll get fat if you eat everything on that plate," Jack teased. "It would be an outright crime to add an ounce to that shape," he grinned, eyeing the sleek, slim lines of her figure.

"Look who's talking," Megan scoffed with a disdainful toss of her head. "I'd strongly suggest you take your own advice. Even without my glasses I can see the definite beginnings of a roll around that *once* slim waist you're so proud of."

"A roll?" Jack repeated in a shocked voice. He held his plate away from him and bent his head, his gaze probing the supposedly offending area of his torso.

Megan's sense of humor got the best of her as she stood back and laughingly viewed his ridiculous posturing. "And they say women are vain."

"You are a coldhearted woman," Jack muttered darkly. "And to pay you back for your little trick, I refuse to shield you from Fred the wimp."

They spotted a vacant table and made their way toward it. "Don't tell me he's here." Megan pulled a long face as she carefully lowered her plate to the table, then sat down.

"In the flesh and trying to hit on every female present." Jack grinned. "I can hardly wait for him to zoom in on you."

"Well, while you're waiting," Megan sweetly smiled, "why don't you trot your loathsome bod over to the bar and get me another glass of wine?"

"Again?" he asked in an irritatingly smug voice, pretending to be shocked at her request.

"Yes," Megan replied off-handedly, her attention focused on the food before her in an effort to identify what she'd put on her plate as well as the choices Jack had made for her. "Going out with you automatically calls for a certain fortification. In this instance it happens to be of the alcoholic variety."

"And to think I brought this on myself," he grinned. One hand reached out and a long finger tapped her nose. "For God's sake, stay put," he cautioned. "You're sitting about three feet from the edge of the pool."

While she was alone, Megan picked at the food and found, to her dismay, that she really wasn't having a good time. Not that Jack wasn't his usual pleasant self, nor was it the party. But in spite of her efforts to let herself go, to relax, she found her thoughts straying to Rhys.

Had he found someone else to have dinner with? Someone not only to spend the evening with, but the night as well?

The frown that marred her smooth brow and the thoughtful set of her lips drew a speculative look from Jack as he returned to the table bearing a drink for each of them.

"Did Fred manage to make a pass at you in the short time I was gone?" he asked.

"What?" Megan looked up questioningly at him, then shook her head and smiled. "No, the wimp hasn't as yet honored me with his presence."

"Then what's the problem?" he persisted. "You haven't been yourself all evening."

Immediately Megan felt contrite. Jack didn't deserve to be treated shabbily. "I'm sorry, I've had a couple of things on my mind. If I promise to do better, will you forgive me?"

Jack, startled that his question had brought about such a reaction, thoughtfully stared into the blue eyes turned on him for a few seconds, then reached out and patted the slim hand resting on the edge of the table. "That's what friends are for. But would you mind smiling once in a while? I'd hate for the eligible ladies at this shindig to think I'm a bore. Hurry up and finish your food," he directed her in a lighter voice. "I want to dance."

That exchange seemed to relax Megan and also set the mood while they finished eating and later as they danced.

After following Jack through several slow numbers and then a last wild and fast one, she pleaded exhaustion and voiced her intention of sitting out the next two or three. Her announcement brought about a great deal of good-natured ribbing that she had a chump for a partner from the small group surrounding them.

Jack gave the hecklers a pained look that also included Megan, then spotted Stacy Owens across the way. His face took on a comically, leering expression and he bounded off in her direction.

Megan laughingly turned and reached for a frosted drink someone had gotten for her, and at the same time felt a large hand clamp like steel fetters around her other wrist.

Even before she swung around, the identity of her assailant was known. No other man, merely by touching her, could cause the soft skin of her nape to prickle with awareness.

"I think this dance is mine," Rhys murmured close to her ear, his breath fanning her cheek.

Unconscious of the interested looks coming from the guests closest to them, Megan followed the pressure of his hand on her wrist, the excitement glowing in her eyes as she raised her velvety blue orbs to meet his dark enigmatic ones.

"This is a surprise," she said in a voice that even to her own ears sounded shaky. God! Even without being able to see him clearly, he was magnificent, she was thinking as her gaze swept over the close-cut dark hair and the immobile features of his face that were as unrevealing as his eyes.

The broad shoulders she'd clung to so eagerly

on other occasions were now clad in a light-weight, dark brown sports jacket worn over a pale beige shirt. Darker beige pants drew attention to his trim waist and flat stomach, and molded the muscled hardness of his strong thighs.

"Really?" The rich huskiness of his voice was as much responsible for sweeping her along to a less crowded spot as was the arm that removed the drink from her unresisting fingers and placed it on a table, then slipped into place around her waist.

"Yes, really," Megan replied breathlessly. "You've obviously met quite a few people since your arrival in Pensacola."

"Oh, I have." Rhys spoke close to her ear, having neatly enfolded her in his arms and against his chest. "But I'm old enough and experienced enough to know that when one has money, one shouldn't set much store by the friendly overtures so eagerly offered."

He settled his stubborn chin against her dark hair, the closeness of him willing her body to follow his lead.

"Aren't you being just a bit critical of people in general and their efforts to make you feel welcome?" Megan asked. Dancing with him seemed to be the most natural thing in the world. There was no shyness on her part at being held so closely. But even if there had been, she knew he would have brushed it aside and done exactly as he pleased.

What was giving her cause for concern,

though, was the slow tantalizing movements of his large hand as it moved over her back from her waist to shoulders, and the way even her bones felt as though they were made of jelly.

"No. I simply refuse to look at the world through rose-colored glasses as you do. Do you honestly believe the Summerses would have invited me if Carl wasn't hopeful of unloading some part of the enormous amount of real estate he's paying taxes on, not to mention the staggering interest he's handing over to the banks on the money he borrowed to buy the land?"

Megan met his dark, cynical gaze with her own thoughtful but fuzzy one. "If you really feel that way, why did you bother to come?"

"You know damn well why I came, Megan, so don't pretend otherwise." The rough edge of his voice belied the seemingly innocent conversation it looked as though they were having. "I learned about the party while playing golf with Carl and Jack. Then when you said you were seeing Jack this evening, I naturally assumed I'd find the two of you here."

"You wouldn't have come otherwise?" something urged her to ask.

"No." His answer was short and to the point. "In my position I'm obligated to do a certain amount of socializing, so when I get the chance to avoid the usual cocktail parties and other social gatherings everyone thinks so important, I gladly do so and with relief."

"Am I suppose to feel guilty or flattered?"

"Neither," he said, and for the first time since his arrival she thought she saw the beginnings of a smile in the depths of his eyes. "I wanted to spend the evening with you so I came to the party. And whether or not you know it, the expression in your face when you turned and looked up at me made enduring this noisy crowd worthwhile."

There didn't seem to be a reply at the moment nor did it appear he was expecting one. Megan simply forgot about Jack and the fact that she was supposed to be with him and the curious looks from some of the other guests. Even Rhys's cynical outlook was momentarily forgotten as the spell and feel and scent of him swept over her and held her prisoner.

That first dance seemed to end almost before it began, as did the second. Before the third started, a faintly amused Jack tapped Rhys on the shoulder.

"If I'd known you planned to sneak in here and try to steal my date, I wouldn't have suggested you drop by."

"She looked lonesome." Rhys grinned, not even bothering to remove his arms still encircling Megan's waist. "You were so wrapped up in the delectable Stacy, I felt it my duty to take pity on your date."

"Pity?" Megan spluttered as she cast a squinty-eyed glare from one grinning face to the other. "Of all the gall!" she exclaimed, stepping back from the warmth of Rhys's body. "I think the two of you deserve each other." With a disgusted toss of her dark head, she neatly stepped around both men, only to come to an abrupt halt when she thought she spotted Fred the wimp headed toward her. Even the poor state of her eyesight couldn't disguise his portly hulk.

"Er, on second thought," Megan began, quickly debating the lesser of the two evils, "since the evening's almost over, I should be generous and allow the two of you what time is left."

Without daring to look at Jack or Rhys, she stepped neatly between them, placing a hand on each of the arms on either side of her. "Shall we stroll over to that charming little table in the corner? We could also ask Stacy to join us. It would make us a happy, charming little foursome," she added tauntingly.

"You must learn to beware of our little gal here, Rhys, when she speaks in that syrupy, sweet voice," Jack warned. "It usually means she's annoyed or"—he caught sight of Fred Knight and grinned—"being pursued by her former flame."

"He is not my former anything!" Megan exclaimed in an angry hiss. She jerked her hands from their arms and took two defiant steps forward, only to be pulled back by a strong grip on her shoulders.

"Take your hands off me," she muttered as she felt Rhys's close presence directly behind her and caught the familiar scent of his cologne.

"And let you disgrace yourself by walking straight into the swimming pool?" he teasingly asked amid the amused chuckles rumbling in his chest. "I think not, Megan. I'm sure there'll be times in the future when I'll be tempted to *throw* you in, but the moment will be private, believe me."

Suddenly she was more than a little annoyed that all during the day when she'd thought him tied up with a backlog of work, he'd been involved in nothing more strenuous than lifting a golf club. Now he was calmly assuming a further-ance of their relationship and that bothered her. She couldn't honestly say why it annoyed her but it did.

"You sound awfully certain you'll get the chance to throw me into the pool, Mr. Warner," she snapped, gamely holding on to the remnants of her annoyance with both men.

"Would you care to place a wager on the out-come, Miss Colby?" he whispered for her ears alone, his lips brushing the pearly pinkness of her lobe.

Megan wished with all her might to be able to ignore him and walk away. It simply wasn't fair that Rhys held so many trumps in his hand while she was left with nothing but her heart and emo-tions, neither of which appeared to be faring too well beneath his close attention.

"Am I to take your silence as a sign of defeat?" he softly taunted her.

"Defeat?" She turned her head up to him, the closeness of his face sending a reckless shiver of excitement through her. "You actually expect me to be at your mercy after meeting me for lunch a couple of times and taking me to dinner three or four times? You should live so long, Mr. Warner.''

"Surely you aren't going to try to make me believe you find me repulsive.''

"Indeed, I am not,'' Megan informed him spiritedly. "But before—'' Suddenly Jack's face floated before her eyes. Lord! She'd never in her entire life committed such a breach in common courtesy, not to mention plain good manners. "Where's Jack?''

"Continuing his pursuit of the lovely Stacy,'' Rhys matter-of-factly informed her. "Why?''

Megan shrugged. "I've never arrived at a party with one man, then spent most of the evening talking and dancing with another.''

"Well, from the looks of things, I'd say he isn't exactly heartbroken,'' Rhys remarked dryly. "He's holding Stacy so close, I doubt a piece of dental floss could be forced between them. Does that revelation particularly bother you?'' he asked gruffly.

"No. In fact I'm quite relieved. He's had his eye on her for some time.''

"So you really were telling the truth, weren't you?''

"I beg your pardon?'' Megan raised her voice in order to be heard over the music that had been turned up to a deafening level. What on earth was he talking about? Better still, why were they having such a personal conversation in a setting where anyone, if they were of a mind, could eavesdrop.

Sensing her discomfort, Rhys cupped her elbow and led her to a secluded table and seated her, then sat down to her right.

"Perhaps now we can hear each other without having to shout."

"Would you please explain that last remark?" Megan asked without preamble, the fiery glitter in her eyes not unnoticed by her companion.

Rhys stared thoughtfully at her, then shrugged. "I obviously misjudged you," he said at last. "You told me your relationship with Jack was strictly platonic but I had my doubts. Now I believe you."

"That's supposed to give me some sort of thrill? Perhaps gladden my poor maiden's heart that you don't consider me a conniving female?" she shot back. He was impossible! No wonder he was divorced. Who the hell would want him?

"That's not at all what I mean and you damn well know it," Rhys growled, his dark brows snapping together above his eyes in a forbidding line.

"Oh? Then pray enlighten me. It should prove interesting," Megan continued on in that annoying way she had when wanting to be particularly perverse. "It's not every day that I'm called a liar by someone who's known me for less than two weeks."

"I'm not so sure that's the problem at all," Rhys told her. "I think you're itching for a fight and anything I say will be met with a prickly reply. I wonder why that is?"

Megan met his gaze as best she could, thinking she'd never felt at such a disadvantage, due to her poor eyesight, as at just that moment. And even though she knew her handicap was minor when compared to others, nonetheless, without her glasses, it kept her from being able to watch the play of emotions that skipped across his face or the expression in his dark eyes that could be so revealing.

"Am I correct, Megan?"

There was a quiet calmness about her as she sought to deal with his question. In addition to feeling ignored during the day, she was also resentful of his attitude toward her friends and women in general. Or was her resentment directed at herself for finding him attractive in spite of his opinion of life and people?

There was total honesty in her eyes that looked across and met his. "I'm really not certain, Rhys. I've never met anyone with as much bitterness inside them as you seem to have. Perhaps I do look at life as you suggested—through rose-colored glasses. Is that so terrible?"

"Only if you refuse to see life as it really is."

She couldn't help but smile at his stubbornness. "Need I point out that ideologically we're poles apart?"

"At the moment, princess, a shared ideology is hardly the most important thing on my mind," he remarked. "When I think of you, when I look at

102

you, my thoughts are totally centered around one single purpose."

"Which is?" The question exploded from her lips without hesitation, one part of her dreading what she would hear, the other part unable to resist that very feminine emotion of wanting to be physically desirable in a man's eye.

"I want you."

CHAPTER SIX

"How flattering, Rhys," Megan replied dryly as she glowered at him. "Your forcefulness in stating your desire reminds me of a farmer selecting the plumpest melon from his garden."

"Believe me, Megan," he smoothly pointed out. "As melons go, you'd probably not make the grade—because of the lack of plumpness, that is. But take heart, honey, I've always preferred my women on the slim side."

"Oh, thank you!" she exclaimed, placing a hand over her heart in a gesture of relief. "It's such a comfort to know that at my age there's still a man out there who, regardless of his age and condition, finds me attractive." She gave a shake of her head and sighed dramatically. "You overwhelm me."

Rhys sat forward, his forearms resting on the

edge of the table, his fingers intertwined as he observed her. "I'd like to turn you over my lap and paddle your cute little behind," he growled.

"Oooh, no," she vigorously shook her head, deliberately assuming an obtuse air. "I don't go in for the kinky stuff, Rhys. That does surprise me, I might add," she stared at him with a straight face. "You hardly seem the type for such antics. Have you ever thought of seeing an analyst?"

"Never," he snapped, "until the last five minutes. No wonder Jack Lindsey doesn't bother to hide his admiration for Stacy Owens. The poor bastard's back is probably still bleeding from the lashings of your sharp tongue."

Megan turned her head in the direction of several couples dancing, one of which she assumed to be Jack and Stacy.

"Is that what you really think? That I lead Jack around by the nose? Well, I hate to disappoint you, but he's no patsy. He does, however, suffer from the same malady you do, namely, that of hoping to entice each woman he fancies into his bed. I only hope he possesses more finesse than your steamroller tactics."

There was a pregnant silence that seemed to stretch interminably. Rhys studied the flashing eyes and gentle beauty of the face before him, a face that had become as familiar to him as his own. There was a glint of admiration in his dark eyes as well. He couldn't remember ever before having been turned down by a woman or told off in such cavalier fashion.

Still fresh in his memory was the feel of her warm, slender body in his arms. Dancing with her had served only to remind him of several evenings before in her apartment and the way she'd responded to him.

His mind seemed to take on a mechanical rapidity as flashes of a pearl-tipped breast, warm against his palm, a hot, moist mouth, and a trembling body, hopscotched through the corridors of his mind.

Was his attraction for her some trick of fate? Some sort of grim retribution for the manner in which he'd dealt with women in the past? Was she, beneath that veneer of honesty, really any different from the others?

Though she was unable clearly to discern his close scrutiny, some innate sense warned Megan that there was more involved in his silent probing than that of a man hopeful of persuading a woman to share his bed.

"Are you ready to leave?" Rhys finally broke the tense silence.

"I'm not sure. Ja—"

"I'm taking you home," he interrupted. "So don't worry about Jack."

"Why?"

"Because now that it's obvious that—"

"I'm not talking about Jack," Megan was stubbornly persistent. "Why do you want to take me home? So far we haven't been able to agree on one single thing. All we seem to do is take careful aim at each other and fire away." She took a deep breath, then let it slowly ease past her lips. "I *have known* couples to be more compatible than we are," she said softly.

All of which fell on deaf ears as Rhys stood and held out his hand to her. Megan hesitated only a moment before allowing her smaller one to be swallowed in his warm grasp.

"Will you please find Jack? I've no intention of leaving here until I've spoken with him. Even a friend deserves some explanation."

"Of course," Rhys agreed so quickly it was all she could do to keep from banging him over the head with the first available weapon. He was getting his way, again, and it annoyed her.

Besides, she thought petulantly as she held his arm and blindly followed his lead, it simply wasn't good for a man to always get his way, at least that was Aunt Bea's philosophy, and Megan agreed.

"The male, from birth," her aunt had counseled her niece early in life, "thinks he's superior in every way to the female. It's up to us women to correct that erroneous idea."

Thus far, Megan wasn't too sure Aunt Bea would approve her handling of Rhys.

Jack, on seeing Megan and Rhys approaching, detached himself from Stacy and stepped forward, a broad grin slowly stealing over his face. "Trouble already?" he asked, amused, noting the mulish set of Megan's features.

"No," she snapped. "I merely wanted to let you know that I'm leaving." She looked beyond him to the hazy outline of Stacy as she sat waiting. "Is she buying your ridiculous story?"

"Don't be nosy, toots," Jack chuckled.

"Oh, I'm not, believe me. But just in case you do fail, don't fling yourself in front of a speeding car. You can simply join forces with Rhys, then the two of you can form a club, write a book. The possibilities are limitless."

Before Jack could do more than laugh, Rhys grasped Megan's arm and determinedly led her across the patio, through the house, and to his car, where he bundled her into the passenger seat.

"Has it occurred to you that we didn't say a word to the hostess?" she flung at him as he got in the car and started the engine.

"With you in your present mood?" Rhys threw her a guarded look. "Had I risked such an encounter, you'd probably have proceeded to lecture her on the evils of sleeping with her husband."

Megan refrained from answering, suddenly finding the entire eposide amusing. "I can occasionally exert some self-control," she informed him dryly. "It's just that I resent being passed around from man to man like a loaf of bread. I also dislike being taken for granted."

"Oh, well, now I understand," Rhys calmly informed her as he maneuvered the car in and out of traffic. "Your ego's been dented and, according to you, I should be an expert on egos—"

"My ego has nothing to do with it," she interrupted. "At least I don't think so," she said thoughtfully. She turned and stared at the huge bulk next to her, irritated that she didn't know him well enough to read the signals he was sending out.

How could she explain that she resented his arrival at the party with seemingly one purpose in mind—that of removing Jack as her escort and assuming that role for himself.

Earlier in the day she'd tensely waited for him to call, her breath catching each time the phone had rung. Those few hours had gone a long way toward helping her see that forming any sort of attachment to Rhys was not the most sensible thing a woman could do.

And yet, later at the party, when she'd felt his touch, Megan knew that regardless of the wisdom of caring for him, there was something in her heart for Rhys. Something she either couldn't or wasn't ready to put a name to.

Face it, her conscience warned, *you resent being manipulated; most people do.*

"Am I still on your black list, or may I come in for a cup of coffee?" The deep voice of the man beside her broke into her thoughts. She looked startled for a moment, then realized the car was stopped and they were parked in front of her apartment.

"I'm sure I'd be better off in the long run if I said you were at the top of my list, but for the time being I've exerted enough energy toward disliking you," Megan bluntly told him.

"As you said earlier, I'm overwhelmed," Rhys rejoined, his tone as flat as hers had been blunt. He got out of the car and came around and opened the door for her.

"Bear in mind that it's a drink I'm offering you, not the use of my bed."

"Of course, Megan, anything you say."

Rather than instilling even the slightest assurance in her that he would cooperate, his reply earned him her most suspicious look.

When they reached her apartment, Rhys cut through what would have been a mad search for the key by deftly plucking the small purse from her hands, locating the key, and unlocking the door.

He opened it with a flourish, then bowed Megan through to the dimly lit room in such an outrageous manner, she had no recourse but to grin at his audacity.

"Ah, a smile," he chortled. "I had begun to think you incapable of such frivolity."

"Don't let it go to your head, buster." Megan flashed him another pert grin. "I'm still annoyed." She brushed by him, not stopping till she reached one overstuffed arm of the sofa. She leaned against the firm support, then lifted first one foot and then the other as she unfastened the tiny buckles and stepped out of her shoes.

Rhys followed and stood patiently by. It was only when she made as though to leave that he stopped her by slipping his arms around her. By taking one step backward, he was on the sofa arm and pulled Megan between his muscled thighs. The unexpected move placed her at eye level with him, her face uncomfortably close to his.

For several moments they simply stared at each other, each dealing with their own private thoughts and the multitude of doubts running through their minds.

It was a new experience being in this particular position, and one Megan could find little fault with.

"Don't you think you've punished me enough for whatever it is you think I've done?" Rhys asked in a barely audible rasp. As he spoke, his arms tightened their hold around her waist, pressing her more intimately against the tautness of his thighs.

Megan absorbed this adjustment of their bodies into her being without feeling threatened in the least. Nor did she panic when she felt the familiar strength of his hand kneading and massaging the knotted muscles in her neck and shoulders.

Without any thought other than a purely spontaneous one, she rested her arms on Rhys's broad shoulders and laced her fingers at the back of his neck. "Believe it or not, punishment hasn't entered into it. I think retaliation is a better word," she grinned sheepishly, her thumb idly brushing back and forth against the dark hair of his nape.

"What did I do to hurt you?" The question and the sincerity behind it gently swept over Megan like a blanket of warmth.

111

"It doesn't matter now." Funny thing was, it really didn't.

"It does to me," Rhys persisted. "The first moment you looked up at me at the party, I saw something that pleased me very much, Megan. But"—he leaned his head forward until his brow was resting against hers—"almost before I knew it, you were hissing and spitting at me like some small furry creature, not to mention the burning looks you blasted me with. So please explain this peculiar habit you have of running hot and cold."

"I do not run hot and cold," she said in spite of the preponderance of evidence against her. Besides, at the moment, she was finding it most difficult to keep his list of trangressions foremost in her thoughts. She much preferred a more physical interchange to this ridiculous conversation he seemed bent on having.

Suddenly Aunt Bea's profound belief reared its helpful head, and Megan hastened to obey the teachings of her elder.

With the ease of a seductress weaving her spell, she disentangled her fingers only to lose them in the crisp thickness of Rhys's hair. With the shape of his head clasped ever so gently between her palms, she eased his face up, then followed with her own, her lips brushing against his like the soft flutter of a floating leaf. The rough sigh of pleasure mixed with surprise that escaped him gave her added confidence.

When this enticing dalliance no longer interested her, Megan began to pay special attention to the sensual fullness of his bottom lip, alternately tracing and nipping at the fullness.

Strange, she thoughtfully mused, caught halfway between her surprise at her daring, and the pleasure she was deriving from Aunt Bea's logical conclusion regarding the male of the species. *I wonder why I've never considered this delightful pastime before?* Then just as quickly the answer flashed through her mind. She'd never wanted to touch, to taste a man, until Rhys came along.

"You went to great lengths to let me know that a drink was all I should expect," he muttered against the softness of her lips that were slowly pushing him to the brink of his control. "Do you have any idea what will happen if you keep this up?"

Megan's mouth moved uncertainly against his, and for the life of her she couldn't think of anything to say. Rhys, who had remained quiescent during this startling but enjoyable experiment on her part, then took command.

Before she could draw back, before she could even guess his intentions, Megan felt herself swung off her feet, her much slighter build being carried downward by Rhys's heavier weight to the cushions of the sofa.

Now he was no longer the tame cat she'd thought, quietly waiting on his leash, but a man with a need and a desire far greater than anything or anyone she'd encountered.

His tongue invaded and became the victor over the dark warmth of her mouth as it darted and plundered, seeking out each tiny treasure revealed to him.

Fingers that had trailed so lazily over her shoulders only moments ago now became insistent as they came in contact with the swollen tips of her breasts through the thin material of the jumpsuit.

When his thirst for her became deeper, Rhys sought the fastenings of the bodice. Finding none, he muttered a sharp expletive, then let his fingertips deftly track the criss-crossed arrangement and slipped his hand inside to cup the weight of one creamy, pink-tipped mound.

The friction of his thumb circling, then flicking her nipple in rapid sequence had Megan arching against him, her head thrown back as she became oblivious to everything but the pleasure of his hands . . . his lips.

When Rhys forsook her lips to pay closer attention to the wildly beating pulse in her throat with his tongue, Megan grasped at his shoulders, her fingers clutching his solidness for support in this swirling, spinning storm of passion that held her in its grip.

She could feel his hands sweeping her from hip to breast, his palms cupping and squeezing her softness, then on to another spot that heretofore had been simple flesh and bone, but beneath his sensitive fingers, became points of desire.

Her body was on fire, screaming out for the caress of hands that had turned into instruments of exquisite torture, alternately soothing and raising to fever pitch the wild crescendo of passion within her.

When suddenly the shards of excitement began to ebb and his hands became less venturesome, Megan fought through the mist of pleasure in an attempt to find the reason for this interruption of ecstasy.

"Every good thing has to end, princess." Rhys's deep voice completed her journey from a world of unbelievable sensual awareness to the harsh glare of the present.

Megan opened her eyes and met his slightly fuzzy brown gaze that pinned her with its careful watchfulness.

"Must you be such a party-pooper?" she asked dreamily. Her slim hand reached up, the oval-tipped fingers skipping along the stubborn line of his jaw. "And another thing, Mr. Warner, this was my show; you had no right to take over."

Rhys made no effort to move his large body that was still keeping her pressed deep into the cushions. He did shift his position enough to wedge one huge fist beneath her chin as he regarded her with amusement. "Little girls shouldn't play with fire, princess. All sorts of accidents can happen."

"I wouldn't call what happened between us an accident, Rhys," she whispered.

"Does that bother you?"

"That we turn each other on? That we're both as wary of each other as two foxes?" At his nod she shook her head. "No. It's just another item to add to the list I'm compiling regarding the elusive Rhys Warner," she teased.

"Why a list?"

"Oh, so that I can compare you with all the other men in my life. There are so many, I have a devil of a time keeping them straight." Her eyes shone mischievously.

"Then why don't we go a step further and finish what we started?" he asked silkily, letting his hand ease up and cover her breast, his fingers carefully cupping the complete fullness. "There'd be no doubt in your mind then as to who will head your little list."

Megan tilted her head to one side in silent contemplation, her lips pursed thoughtfully. "No, I don't think we're ready for the next phase right at this point, do you?"

Rhys also seemed to have his doubts, in spite of the image he'd created over the years. "Strangely enough, I'm of two minds regarding the subject. Making love to you would be very enjoyable, and if you say the word, I'll certainly not quibble. But"—and then he frowned, his face unreadable—"my intuition tells me that now isn't the time. I've always come out a winner when I've followed my intuition."

It was as though a hand reached inside her chest and gripped her heart, or so it felt to Megan as his words hit her. Who would ever have thought that Rhys Warner, reputed playboy and certified heartbreaker, would ever resist an opportunity to add another scalp to his belt?

"Thank you," she finally managed. "I won't insult you by saying I'm not attracted to you, for I am. You"—she tapped him on his chest—"are a very sexy man. You could have pushed us over the brink this evening, but you didn't. I like that trait in you, Rhys, even if you are a bully in other ways."

"Then I hope you won't mind doing one tiny favor for me," he murmured, his lips suddenly swooping and tasting hers.

"What?" she asked against the thrill of excitement that raced through her veins.

"Tear up your damn list, princess," he growled. His fingers caught her chin and held it as his dark eyes burned into her warm blue ones. "I don't make concessions like I did this evening for my health. Do you get my drift?"

"On one condition," Megan smiled.

"Name it."

"That you never put a round of golf before me again."

"Never put a rou—I don't believe it!" he stared incredulously. "So that's what's been wrong with you. You thought I was taking you for granted?" he asked curiously.

"Something like that, and I didn't like it."

"So I noticed, princess, so I noticed."

"Agreed?"

"Agreed," he replied and quite properly sealed the bargain with an appropriate kiss.

CHAPTER SEVEN

Sunday proved to be an interesting day, even if its supposedly restful reputation was broken from time to time by the clashes of will, not to mention of temper, that flared between Megan and Rhys.

The evening before had stretched, enjoyably so, into the wee hours of the morning. Rhys had seemed in no hurry to leave, and the hours flew by as they talked and argued and kissed, then started all over again.

At the door, as he was leaving, his pointed "*I will* call you tomorrow" brought a grin to Megan's face.

"See," she teased. "An old dog can indeed be taught new tricks."

The remark was meant to bring a reaction from him, and it did, in the form of her being crushed against the solid wall of his chest, her arms pinned to her sides.

"Remember one thing, princess," Rhys grinned down at her. "This old dog can only be teased for just so long. Each cute remark, each tiny jab at my tough hide, will be remembered, and one day soon I'll collect what's due me. What do you have to say to that?"

"Why, only that you talk too much, if you get my drift," she replied daringly.

"Unfortunately I do," he sighed, his mouth descending on hers and kissing her into a state of wobbly knees and hands wildly clutching at the lapels of his jacket. He raised his head and stared at her. "I'm sure somewhere down the road I'll learn why I keep heaping coals of torment upon my head. At the moment, however, I think I'm crazy as hell."

He thrust Megan back a safe distance, opened the door, and stepped into the corridor, then closed the door with a resounding bang.

A bemused expression crept over her face as she stood staring at the solid panel of wood. In spite of his bouts of suspicion and his distrust of people in general, she'd learned one very important thing about Rhys Warner. The man had character.

He had pressed and she'd bent. Had he pushed, she would have crumpled.

Somehow this different and revealing insight into his complex personality brought about a sense of compassion for Rhys. He'd obviously suffered hurt upon hurt in his childhood that had left him emotionally scarred. Could she erase those scars and teach him to trust again? Dare she open her heart to the risk involved, especially if she failed?

These questions and others equally perplexing stayed on her mind as she went through her nightly ritual of brushing her hair, washing her face, and cleaning her teeth.

But instead of spending hours tossing and turning and finding sleep as elusive as a rare butterfly, when she did go to bed Megan dropped off immediately to dream of Rhys.

Sunday morning, the few hours of the week proclaimed by Megan since childhood to be her very own, was usually spent sleeping in. When she would finally get out of bed, it was to pad barefoot to the kitchen, put on a pot of coffee, retrieve the morning paper, then settle down in quiet solitude.

It was a routine that seldom varied. Her family and closest friends had been subjected on occasions to an example of her temper if this routine varied, and had no desire to repeat the process.

On this particular Sunday morning, however, there was no one to warn Rhys that disturbing Megan was tantamount to awakening a hibernating bear.

Thus the ungodly pounding on her door at the unheard hour of eight ten caused a bleary-eyed Megan to spring into a jackknife position in the middle of her bed.

"I don't believe this," she muttered, her expression dark.

When it became evident that her caller wasn't about to desist and quietly steal away, Megan flounced out of bed. She groped blindly for her robe, shrugging her arms into the sleeves, and jerking the soft, tie belt into a knot as she stalked from the bedroom.

She crossed the living room in the same determined stride, muttering imprecations of doom and various forms of torture upon the head of the person responsible for disturbing her rest.

The doorknob was firmly grasped and the door flung open to reveal Rhys, leaning unconcernedly against the doorjamb. The best she could make out, he was casually dressed in faded jeans, a light blue pullover shirt, and a pair of track shoes.

"Yes?" Megan stonily inquired of him, not budging an inch from her position smack in the middle of the opening nor offering the least encouragement that he was welcome.

"Good morning, sunshine," Rhys said cheerfully, chuckling at the wrathful, sleep-warmed spitfire glaring at him.

"That's questionable," she flatly declared. "I *never* receive guests before noon on Sunday mornings."

"My, my," he laughed outright at her peevish tone. "You really are a grouch this morning, aren't you?"

"Yes. And every other morning as well. I abhor chatty people."

"Oh, well." He pushed himself upright. "We all have our little problems, don't we?" He reached out and gently but firmly moved her aside, then came in and closed the door behind him.

"Weren't you listening?" she demanded.

"Certainly," Rhys replied calmly. "But knowing what a sweet, engaging person you are, I'm sure you don't mean to appear so ungracious."

Before she could do more than flail him with a withering look, he caught her to him and dropped a hard kiss on her lips, then had the audacity to grin at her frowning countenance.

"I also don't care for physical contact in the morning," she remarked icily, trying to ignore the traitorous response that was springing to life within her body. Damn him! It simply wasn't fair.

She was never at her best early in the morning, and no one became involved in a skirmish with a man like Rhys until their head was clear and they were in top form.

"Then I'm afraid you're going to have to learn to like it, sweetheart." He seemed to be getting a fiendish delight in annoying her, considering he hadn't loosened his arms that were still holding her. "I do like contact, especially with you. I'm also hungry."

"Now, let's get some ground rules laid down, Mr. Warner." Megan tried to remain stern, which was becoming more difficult by the second. "I don't do windows nor do I cook huge breakfasts for inconsiderate louts with big appetites."

"No problem. You go get a shower and wash away the cobwebs while I cook breakfast." He eased her back and let his warm gaze travel the length of her, his hands gliding to the gentle curves of her body beneath the robe. "I'll even serve you in bed," he added huskily.

"I just bet you would." Megan gave in to the charisma of him and smiled. "But are you sure it's my appetite you'd be concerned with?"

"No," he admitted unabashedly. "But I guarantee you'd never glare at me again in the morning."

"You have an answer for everything, don't you?" Megan asked curiously, part of her wondering what it would be like if she were to agree with his suggestion. Could she let him make love to her today . . . perhaps tomorrow, then calmly turn away when he moved on to someone else?

"Yes, I don't believe in leaving things to chance. There are times when you have to make events happen," Rhys murmured, seeing the doubts and indecision flickering in her eyes.

Damn! He wanted to trust her, wanted to believe she was different. But he'd seen too damned much to completely open himself to anyone again.

Although, his sixth sense warned him, Megan Colby, with the quicksilver smile and the laughing eyes, was slowly placing him in a position he'd avoided like the plague for many years.

"I hate to be a wet blanket, Rhys"—Megan regarded him with feigned innocence—"and I

really do want to thank you for the . . . er
. . . offer. It's the best one I've had this morning,
but I'll pass. You may, however, prepare breakfast." She grandly gave her consent as if bestow-
ing a great honor upon him. "I suddenly find I'm
starving."

After breakfast, which was huge and caused
Megan to groan as she consumed more calories
in that one meal than she normally did in an
entire day, Rhys insisted on sharing the cleaning
up.

It was somewhat amusing to see a man of his
size, not to mention his wealth, wearing her one
and only frilly apron, his tanned forearms covered with soapsuds. Was this the real Rhys, or
was he willing to go to any lengths to get his way?
Was the game of deception he accorded all
women as being masters of relegated to the feminine sex? Wasn't he, by exerting his charms and
expertise at seduction, just as guilty?

No, Megan thought as she silently regarded the
giant at her sink. He didn't play fair at all. He
bullied, teased, and totally disregarded her pro-
tests, carrying them both along on his strength,
and, most of all, making her like it as he did so.

The remainder of the day was spent as the
morning had been, with Rhys calmly taking over.
There was a picnic, which he'd had prepared, on
the beach. Later, a leisurely drive along the coast,
and finally a quiet evening spent in her apartment
listening to soft music as they sprawled on the
sofa sipping wine.

For Megan it was as though each thing they did, each word that passed between them brought them closer to an inevitable reckoning. A reckoning that she was awaiting with curious anticipation and, at the same time, she was dreading.

She wasn't ignorant of the chemistry or to the reluctance that seemed to dictate the moods between them. But was this reluctance on both their parts a subtle warning of fate? That if they ignored it and plunged headlong into an affair, the consequences would far outweigh the moments of pleasure?

"Why the wistful sigh?" Rhys asked. Megan was cuddled against his chest and his arms were wrapped protectively around her.

The music, soft in the background, and the effect of the wine had woven a lacy veil of disquiet over her. She was content but . . .

"I guess it's wishful thinking." She wiggled around so that she could see his face. "Haven't you ever enjoyed something and didn't want it to end?" It wasn't quite the truth, but her real feelings were too new, too personal to reveal.

Rhys stared down at her for what seemed like an incredibly long time, his shuttered gaze safely concealing his thoughts from her. When Megan began to fidget beneath this thoroughly unnerving scrutiny, he captured her neck in a warm clasp and held her still. "Will you forgive me, princess, if I don't believe you?"

Instead of waiting for an answer Megan didn't

have, he let his lips hover over hers, almost but not quite touching. The tension in the air was like invisible magnets holding them suspended in space.

She heard a sound remarkably like a half sigh, half moan, before she realized it had come from her.

"Oh, you witch." Rhys gave a shuddered groan and opened his mouth possessively over hers. His tongue greedily scoured the tiny space that welcomed him, reacquainting itself with each millimeter of softness as he sipped and caressed.

He ached for the feel of her against him, and thrust his hands beneath the knit top she was wearing to run his palms repeatedly over a satiny smooth back and shoulders. The impediment of the fragile scrap of her bra was unfastened and swept aside, leaving bare the proud thrusts of soft, inviting breasts.

When his thumbs scraped the tiny tips before cupping first one gentle weight and then the other, Megan stiffened against the spiraling tongue of desire nipping at her being.

Her lungs felt ready to burst from the breath she'd been holding in anticipation. He was caressing her so provocatively that there wasn't a thing she could or wanted to do about it except give and feel and share in the overwhelming desire enveloping them.

"I want to make love to you, Megan," Rhys breathed against the tender side of her neck, the words coming from his mouth in short, labored gasps as his lips nipped and teased their way to her ear. "You are slowly driving me out of my mind."

He drew back, his hands leaving her softer, more feminine curves to frame her face as his thumbs stroked her eyebrows, the outward lilt of her eyes. They brushed over her small, straight nose, then softly caressed the fullness of her lips.

"I need to see more of you than just dinner, then an hour or two of frantic necking on your sofa," he rasped. "I want you in my bed every night . . . I want to see you moving about my home, my bedroom."

The feeling of ecstasy that had bathed her in its soothing glow slowly turned to cautious reality as she stared at him, as his words penetrated the curtain of well-being that he'd so expertly erected about her.

He wanted. *He* needed. But what about *her*? She wasn't some teenager eager to grasp a few moments, even weeks of happiness brought about by a certain mood or a certain need. Nor was she angling for a proposal of marriage. But when and if she and Rhys made love, she wanted it to be more than a challenge for him. His hands and lips transmitted one message, but his eyes, his mood, told her another story.

"Are you asking me to move in with you, Rhys?" The question slipped past lips that now resented the feathery whisperings of his thumb.

Stop it! she wanted to scream out, but restrained herself. He hadn't hidden his views, and if she felt betrayed, then she had no one but herself to blame.

"Don't tell me you're shocked by the suggestion?"

"No, not shocked," she replied. "More surprised. Does this mean that you no longer suspect me of covert dealings where men are concerned?"

"Don't make an issue out of this, Megan," he warned her, dropping back against the sofa and staring at her.

She caught the edge of her top and pulled it back in place, then reached for her glasses and slipped them on, this latter action thrusting his scowling features into focus.

She drew her feet beneath her, then turned so that she was facing him. "Why not?" she demanded. "It's not often that I'm asked to share a man's bed. A man who's willing to sleep with me, but who doesn't trust me. If I agreed to your suggestion, Rhys, what sort of person would that make me? What about my emotions, my feelings, if and when you find you couldn't change?"

"Has anyone ever told you that you talk too damn much?" he snapped as he reached for her and hauled her against him. "Can't you forget about trust and all those other restrictions rattling around in your head and let us enjoy this chance that's been given us?"

Megan squirmed free of his hold. Now that she'd started this particular argument, she had no intention of letting him wiggle out of it by a further display of his ability to disarm her.

"It's not my head that's in question, Mr. Warner," she pointed out spiritedly. "You're the one who thinks there's a spook behind every tree in your life and that each woman you meet will bring about your downfall through some bizarre act of betrayal."

"All right, all right," Rhys lashed out. "So I'm a suspicious bastard. What does that have to do with us making love, for heaven's sake?"

"Plenty," Megan coolly informed him. "I don't make a practice of going to bed with every man I date. So naturally"—she eyed him meanly—"being the uncomplicated female I am, I would like to think of the experience when it does happen as being a meaningful one. Not my body being used simply as a means of gratification for some man's lust," she added without batting an eye.

"Lust, hell!" he snorted. "You wanted me just as deeply as I wanted you."

"I'm not denying it," Megan tried for a calm tone. "In fact, Rhys, if you ever get your thinking straightened out, give me a call. Otherwise no thanks."

"Mmm, seems to me your stragegy is a little different from some of the others, but with the same goal in mind—that of snaring a rich husband," he scowlingly delivered the insult. "Were you planning to wait until I was a *sure thing* to also

129

drop a few hints regarding some costly trinkets you would just *love* to have?"

Megan couldn't believe her ears. Where women were concerned he was like a stubborn mule equipped with overlapping blinkers. With his particular problem of being totally narrow-minded, nothing short of an atom bomb could break through the granitelike hardness of his head.

As she sat staring at this man whom she had come to love simply and without a single endearing quality on his part, an idea began to take root in the fertile ground of her mind. An idea so outrageous she could barely keep from laughing.

If he's incapable of recognizing honest feelings and emotions when he sees them, then I'll really give him something to raise his black brows about.

"I had hoped it wouldn't be necessary to hint, Rhys," she informed him in her best gold-plated bitch voice. "However, I hadn't counted on you being quite so tight-fisted. Remember the old adage about a woman not being able to live by peanut butter alone. A bracelet here, a diamond pendant there . . ." She smiled sweetly. "Nothing gaudy, but I'm sure you understand that with the inflationary times, a woman has to think of the future."

"Of course," he agreed tonelessly through lips that had suddenly gone colorless. "How remiss of me not to have considered this affair from all angles."

"Don't worry." Megan stressed the last word,

placing a reassuring hand on his arm and smiling at him. "I'm confident you'll correct this small, er, oversight and make our *affair* well worth my while."

From that moment till she saw him out, Megan could easily have closed her eyes and imagined herself in Siberia, so cold was Rhys's frigid tone of conversation. A good-night kiss apparently proved more than he could offer.

After he'd gone, Megan busied herself with returning the wineglasses to the kitchen, wondering as she did, if she'd goaded him too much. Had she pointed the finger of ridicule once too often?

She was certain that to a great extent the trip to Atlanta the following day would lose some of its excitement because of the coolness that existed between them when Rhys said good night. Hopefully, seeing her family would go a long way toward easing the pain she was feeling.

CHAPTER EIGHT

The first thing Megan did after checking into her hotel and being shown to her room was to call home.

Aunt Bea, usually preparing dinner at the time Megan called, answered the phone on the first ring.

"I can almost smell the aroma of your kitchen over the telephone, Aunt Bea. How are you?"

"Megan?" the older woman questioned excitedly. "Are you in town?"

"Yes, I am. And if all goes well, I plan on spending tomorrow night with you and Dad."

"Well, I should hope so," her aunt replied shortly. "I've been cooking all day in hopes you would call. Have you spoken with Francis?"

"No. I called you first. Dad's usually so busy, I hate to disturb him. So"—Megan pulled out a pillow from beneath the spread and settled herself comfortably against the headboard—"tell me the latest gossip."

Now, if there was anything close to Aunt Bea's heart, it was gossip. She absorbed it like a sponge, sorted through it with the precision of a machine, then labeled and stored it away in her mind like a computer. Megan had pushed the correct button, and for thirty minutes or so was regaled with each and every incident of the Colby clan since her last visit.

"Will Ian be there tomorrow evening?" she asked the first chance she got to break into the lengthy monologue.

"He's been invited. Your brother is remarkably like you when it comes to showing up for family gatherings," Beatrice remarked in her blunt way. "Hopefully he'll find time to put in an appearance."

Not wanting to become involved in an argument or endure a stern lecture, Megan quickly brought the conversation to an end by promising to arrive promptly the following afternoon.

Next she dialed Ian's office, and after exchanging pleasantries with his secretary and asking her not to reveal the identity of the caller, she was put through to her brother.

"How would you like to take a beautiful, exciting woman to dinner?" she asked in a throaty tone as soon as he answered.

"Mmm," he mused in a deep voice. Megan had no trouble at all seeing in her mind the dancing amusement in his eyes that were as blue as her own. "What's it worth to you to be seen with a successful broker?"

"Still thinking rather highly of yourself, aren't you, big brother?" She fell easily into the familiar exchange that was part of the deep affection between them.

"How can I not, brat, when there's a line of women backed up for blocks just waiting to see my handsome face."

"Aaah, now I know I'm really home," she chuckled. "It's so refreshing to know that you're still the same chauvinist you've always been. You haven't, however, answered my question. Can you have dinner with me?"

"It will be my pleasure, brat." She gave him the name of the hotel and he told her to be ready promptly at seven o'clock.

"That gives me only forty-five minutes," she spiritedly reminded him. "I have a shower, war paint, and panty hose to wade through."

"Don't bother gilding the lily, I'll even escort you in your natural state. But for heaven's sake wear your glasses. The last time I took you out, you got lost on the way to the ladies' room."

"Gee, it's so comforting to be reminded of one's small failings in such a gentle fashion," she sweetly replied, then dropped the receiver back into its cradle.

Not being one by nature to dawdle, Megan quickly undressed and headed for the shower. As she felt the warmth of the water lift some of the weariness from her body, she admitted to herself the reason for calling Ian.

He had always been the favorite of her four brothers. Not that the others were mean or uncaring, they weren't. But Ian had always taken special pains to see that the "brat" was looked after. With their father's practice demanding so much of his time, it was Ian who taught her to ride a bicycle, to swim, and all the other triumphs that were so important in her young life.

He'd shouted and yelled and threatened to throttle her in true Colby fashion the times she misbehaved, but he'd also, on more than one occasion, taken a frightened little girl into his bed when a thunderstorm or a bad dream threatened her small world.

Now Megan found herself turning to him again, seeking his advice and subconsciously his approval where Rhys Warner was concerned.

Time passed quickly and she was concentrating on getting her eye makeup just so when there was a sharp knock on her door. With a mouthed oath at the interruption, Megan made one last sweep with the tiny brush, then turned and headed toward the door.

At the same moment she called out, "Who is it?" she was peering through the peephole at Ian. She opened the door and attempted to strike a critical pose because he was early, but her happiness at seeing him was too much. "I still have ten minutes," she grinned before throwing herself into his outstretched arms.

Ian chuckled, his arms encircling her and holding her against his chest. "Propriety, brat, propriety. You're a successful career woman now. A visit from your older brother is supposed to be handled with a minimum of fuss while you nail my obnoxious presence with a suspicious glare."

"Need I tell you what you can do with your propriety?" she asked, giving him a noisy kiss on the cheek before stepping back. Megan let her gaze travel over him, then back to his face and hair, where she saw the first faint sprinkling of gray shining boldly among the dark hair at his temples.

"Handsome, distinguished," she quipped. "Aren't you ever going to marry?"

"Perhaps," Ian grinned as he turned her around and gave her a gentle push. "At the moment I'm still enjoying my bachelor existence. You wouldn't believe the number of women eager to make life pleasant for me."

"Enough." Megan held up one hand. "I get the picture, and I don't mind telling you that I think you're a first-class rat. You bear a strong resemblance to someone else I know. Someone who's equally obnoxious."

The restaurant was noted for its excellent food and was not on the beaten tourist path. Megan relaxed in her chair and smiled at her brother. "I approve your choice, Mr. Colby. This is perfect. But hasn't there been extensive remodeling? I know that attractive loft area is new."

"About five years ago to be exact," Ian said. "Would you like something to drink before we order?"

"White wine, please. Anything else will leave me with a woolly head, and I need all my wits about me tomorrow."

Ian gave the waiter their order for drinks, then turned his full attention on Megan. "Are you in some sort of trouble, brat?"

She stared at him across the small table, the flickering candle in the center softening the irregular features of his face. It was a face that seemed curiously familiar to another one irrevocably stamped in her memory. All angles and planes that came together haphazardly but nice.

"I'm in love with a man who, I honestly believe, has never trusted a woman in his life. I'm unhappy away from him, and when we're together we do nothing but fight, figuratively speaking. In a nutshell, brother dear, I'm miserable."

Ian mulled over this rather surprising bit of information, then asked, "Does he love you?"

"He doesn't know the meaning of the word," Megan sighed. "Circumstances, events from his past, have truly left him with an outlook on life and on women that is cynical and harsh. And yet, I've seen him let his guard slip. Even caught a glimpse of the person he could be. I've"—she hesitated, suddenly becoming shy—"I've known gentleness from him and a certain warmth. He isn't a brute."

The waiter arrived with their drinks at that moment. Ian waited until he was gone, then asked, "Just how far has this relationship gone?"

"I haven't slept with him, if that's what you're asking. Not because I haven't wanted to, but because of . . ." She shook her head. "I don't understand Rhys or myself. We're both like two people needing a life-saving drug, but too afraid to risk something that hasn't been tried and proved. We're both so damn cautious, we're almost paranoid."

"Did you say Rhys?"

"Yes. Rhys Warner. He's head of Lodestar Inc. Pensacola has become a temporary base of operation for him. I met him through Jack Lindsey. Have you heard of him?"

Ian nodded. "He has quite a reputation. Some say he's ruthless, but I think the general consensus is that whatever he touches turns to gold. He's the sort of man others are always anxious to know, hoping to ride his coattails in for an easy buck."

He studied Megan for several seconds, catching a glimpse of the vulnerability etched in the fleeting expressions that skipped across her face and in the blue depths of her eyes.

"He's tough, honey. And I can't honestly say I'm pleased. There's a certain reputation that's synonymous with his name where women are concerned. Stories, I grant you, that are only hearsay, but stories nevertheless. Be careful."

"I will," Megan assured him, and then wondered why that particular phrase sounded so out

138

of place when referring to Rhys. She'd been careful, hadn't she? Careful to shield her true feelings from him. Careful to point out that his wealth wasn't important. Careful of this, careful of that. Damn! She devoutly hoped she never heard the word again.

Rather than lecturing on steering clear of Rhys, Ian skillfully kept the conversation on amusing stories regarding the family. The fact that she would be an aunt in the coming months was a pleasant surprise, and one that Aunt Bea had failed to pass on.

"How did she miss telling me?" Megan laughingly asked.

"Because Ed and Susie want to announce it tomorrow evening at dinner," Ian explained. "I happened to be having lunch with him yesterday when Susie joined us. She was about to burst with excitement and lost little time in letting us know why. I thought poor Ed would pass out."

"He was pleased, wasn't he?"

"As punch. But you must remember, brat, he only took the matrimonial plunge a year ago." He grinned rakishly. "Fatherhood has a way of setting a seal of permanency on the union."

"Is that what you're avoiding, Ian?" Megan carefully posed the question. "Believe it or not, you and Rhys remind me a great deal of each other. You sail blithely along, adding notches to your bedpost with all the gusto of a gunfighter in the Old West."

"Has your friend Rhys ever thought of having

your jaws wired shut?" he asked deliberately. "It's a marvelous means of keeping that wicked tongue of yours still."

"I have a feeling when and if the two of you meet, you'll get along famously. He's as unprincipled as you."

By the time Ian saw her to the door of her hotel room, Megan had regained some of the spark usually present in her carefree personality. Not that her problems concerning Rhys were any closer to being solved, but she'd at least gotten away from the confusion of her thoughts for a few hours.

Paul Chandler, chairman of the board of Meta Electronics, proved to be a very discerning individual. After ten minutes in his presence Megan felt like tucking him into her hip pocket and taking him home with her. He was short and stocky, with a face that immediately had one seeing him in a Santa Claus suit.

His eyes indeed twinkled, and if the growth atop his receding hairline was thin, it only added to his overall charm. He possessed the ability to make one feel one was the most important person in the entire world.

Although, as he listened to excerpts from the presentation she'd given him and began asking questions, Megan realized he hadn't been given his position on a silver platter. He'd earned it.

For three long hours they went at it, with Megan at times wanting to scream with frustration at the seemingly nitpicking questions he kept tossing at her. Questions that, to one not involved in industrial development, would have seemed frivolous, but were vital when a plant was being considered and millions of dollars hung in the balance.

´From Santa Claus, Paul Chandler ran the gamut of personalities, including Attila the Hun! But once they'd finished, Megan knew she'd dealt with an expert and hadn't done badly herself. Her private thoughts were echoed when Paul rose smilingly to his feet.

"You're a hell of a fine I. D. man . . . oops . . . woman," he chuckled. "The organization you represent obviously picked a winner when they went with you, Miss Colby. If you ever think of changing jobs, I'd appreciate you giving me a call."

Megan quite naturally basked in the warm words of praise and thanked him. Hopefully she'd done her job well enough that in a few weeks she could announce that Meta Electronics would be expanding to Pensacola.

"Can you join me for lunch?" he asked.

"Certainly," she smiled. "But I'd think by now you would have heard enough about Pensacola and its sellable points."

"Who said anything about Pensacola?" he grinned conspiratorially. "Anytime I get a chance to take a lovely young lady to lunch, I automatically put business on hold."

"Er, doesn't she mind?" Megan nodded toward the smiling brunette in the photograph that occupied a place of honor on his desk.

Paul glanced from the photograph to Megan and smiled. "I'm well shackled, I assure you. But I'm not blinkered, and I have permission to look."

"In that case, Mr. Chandler, I'd be delighted to have lunch with you."

It was as they turned the corner from the shorter corridor that led from Paul Chandler's office and entered the longer one that ended at a bank of elevators, that Megan came to an abrupt halt, a sharp exclamation of surprise escaping her.

"Is something wrong?" Paul quickly asked, his gaze following hers to the elevator.

"I'm, er, no, nothing is wrong," she smiled weakly. "I thought I recognized the man who just got on that elevator. Obviously I was mistaken."

But all through lunch, at which Paul Chandler was his most charming, Megan couldn't erase from her mind the sight of a pair of broad shoulders or the arrogant thrust of a dark head. Was it Rhys she saw entering the elevator? Or was she becoming so possessed with him that she saw him in every man of similar height and build?

After lunch Megan returned to the hotel, packed, and met Ian in the lobby.

"Is this all?" he asked, taking the one piece of luggage that she carried. "I thought all you high-powered female executives traveled with an entire wardrobe."

"Very cute." She glared up at him. "We can't

142

be bothered with tons of luggage. All our energies have to be focused on outsmarting the overbearing men we're forced to deal with."

"Still on your high horse, I see," he grunted as they left the lobby and headed for his car parked at the curb. "Did your morning fizzle out?"

"Actually, I think it went very well."

"Then why the long face?"

"I honestly don't know," Megan openly confessed as she got in the car. "I thought I saw—" She paused, then looked out the window to her right and sighed. "Forget it. I've spent so many hours on this presentation, I'm punchy. What I need is a heavy dose of Aunt Bea's bluntness to set things in perspective again."

"It's nice you feel that way, 'cause that's exactly what you'll get." Ian grinned.

Times changed—styles in clothing came and went. But Aunt Bea merely thumbed her nose at it all and calmly went her own way. If anything, she had become more irascible than ever, although Megan knew from experience that grouchiness and a short temper were merely a front behind which her aunt hid her true feelings. Beatrice Lange simply was one of those people who was afraid to let the world know she was a warm, loving human being.

Her family knew it, though, through her efforts to dictate their lives, the telephone calls they could expect if visits were too long in coming, and by the special meals cooked on birthdays and other events—little things that spoke louder than words of a love hidden in a person's heart and struggling to free itself.

Megan hadn't been in the house ten minutes before she found herself being ordered around as though she were nine years old instead of twenty-nine. She fell in with her aunt's autocratic manner wholeheartedly. It was nice for a change to be told what to do and it also kept her busy enough that her thoughts didn't have time to dwell on Rhys.

Although the more she listened to Aunt Bea, Megan couldn't help but wonder if the dear woman and Rhys were related. The two of them were tarred with the same brush when it came to revealing their true feelings, and the little matter of trusting people.

"Haven't you found a man yet, miss?" The older woman asked the question in her abrupt and abrasive fashion during the time she was turning out three different desserts, and her niece was dutifully trotting back and forth to the dining room, setting the large table for dinner.

"Er, several, Aunt Bea," Megan replied evasively, her mouth quirking amusedly at the no-frills-attached question. "But they all say I'm too opinionated."

"Then you must learn temperance, child, when dealing with a man. But only with the one man you've set your cap for. It never hurts to once in a while let your guard down. You might occasionally go so far as to pretend to listen to whatever it is that interests the pompous ass. Although I really can't blame you if you find that particular aspect unacceptable."

"Are you suggesting I make concessions in order to catch a husband, Aunt Bea?" Megan asked, finding it the most difficult thing in the world not to laugh.

Her aunt stood ramrod straight and pushed the tiny, gold-framed glasses higher on her nose. Not a hair on her silver head was out of place, and the crisp dress she wore complimented a remarkably slim figure for a woman of seventy-two.

She turned and stared at Megan. "There are concessions, Megan, and there are concessions. You must learn to choose the ones that will cause you the minimum of time and effort."

"Is that what you did with Uncle Walt?" Megan asked curiously.

"Walter was a rare man, my dear. I can only hope you will be as lucky. He encouraged me in everything I attempted. Unfortunately I was raised under the misguided teachings that a woman was put here merely to please man. I had no vocation. So quite naturally I channeled my hopes and aspirations to furthering Walter's career. The academic life was good to us."

Before Megan could comment, the phone rang. "Would you get that, dear? It's probably one of your sisters-in-law. They're both feather-heads who think the telephone was invented solely for the purpose of long, meaningless conversations."

Megan obediently hurried to the hall, thinking as she did, that her views regarding her brothers' wives weren't far removed from her aunt's. Which wasn't altogether a comforting thought, she reflected grimly.

She picked up the receiver. "Hello?" Her voice was brisk and pleasant as she prepared for a siege.

"Did your meeting go well with Meta Electronics?" Rhys asked.

Megan felt the air rushing from her lungs as though someone had suddenly wrapped their arms around her and squeezed. Her legs began to shake, and the hand holding the receiver started to tremble.

"Rhys? Are you in Atlanta?" She eventually got out the question in a voice that wasn't nearly as steady as she would have liked.

"Yes and yes," he chuckled, the husky timbre of his voice rushing through the miles of copper and steel to gently wash over her. "I had business in the area, so I thought I'd call and see how your appointment went. Are you really surprised?"

"In view of the way you left my apartment last night, I honestly don't know," she admitted. "How long will you be staying?"

"Until I see you. Will you have dinner with me?"

"Oh, dear," Megan exclaimed anxiously. "If you knew my Aunt Bea, you wouldn't suggest such a thing. She's planning on having the entire Colby clan for dinner this evening."

"I see," he responded in that flat nuance Megan knew so well.

"Why don't you join us?" she asked without even thinking of what she was saying.

"I'd be happy to. What time?" he quickly accepted, seeming to recognize the invitation had been spontaneous and she might withdraw it if given time.

"Around six? That'll give you time to meet everyone." She hesitated, then plunged in. "Are you sure you want to do this, Rhys? My family can be a bit overwhelming. I mean, there are so many of us."

"I'll be there, Megan, at six. Frankly, I'm not too concerned about your family, overwhelming or not. But if it's the only way to see you, then I'll make the best of it. And Megan?"

"Yes?"

"Don't worry about me embarrassing you. When forced, I can be quite human."

When Megan replaced the receiver, she found to her dismay that her palms were damp with perspiration and her knees were still as wobbly as a newborn colt's. "You poor sap," she muttered disgustedly. "You wanted to hold out for bells, and all you've gotten is a continuous feeling that closely resembles a virus."

True love was fast becoming as welcome as a pain in the buns!

Megan sat at one end of the old-fashioned swing on the large back porch that overlooked the pool, and eyed the man responsible for her bouts of sweaty palms, wobbly knees, and the feeling of being cast adrift when away from him. She was further annoyed by Edward's wife sitting next to her, giving a play by play of the exciting early weeks of pregnancy.

Megan tuned her out, then focused her whole attention on Rhys. Rhys Warner, expert manipulator of people, was weaving a spell of cordiality, charm, and wit so successfully about her family that at any moment Megan expected to see the pope appear and canonize St. Rhys!

Even Ian, who'd confessed his less than enthusiastic approval of Rhys when Megan first told him of their relationship, appeared on the friendliest of terms.

When her sister-in-law finally gave up on getting any but the shortest responses from Megan, she headed for Aunt Bea and, hopefully, a more responsive audience.

Rhys, though seemingly involved in a conversation with several of the men, excused himself and walked over to take the seat beside Megan.

"Why the dark expression, princess?" His unfathomable gaze read the signs of displeasure so evident in her face.

Megan stared thoughtfully at him, wondering why he had to be the one man who appealed to her. Why couldn't it have been some poor, uncomplicated sap with an average background, and nothing more complicated in his life than his career and his love for the woman in his life?

148

"I can't help but wonder what sort of perverse pleasure you're getting by appearing to be such a nice guy to my family?"

"Is that what you really think, Megan?"

"Can you prove me wrong? I've seen that look in your eyes that lets me know when you're putting on an act. I've also seen it here, this evening. The expressions of annoyance, quickly shuttered—the smile that doesn't quite reach your eyes."

She wasn't prepared for the smile that tugged at his sensuous mouth. He'd just been insulted; why wasn't he angry? It would be a far simpler reaction to deal with than him grinning at her like a bloody idiot!

"Have I been promoted to your personal court jester?" she snapped.

"You please me, yes. For in spite of that wicked tongue with which you constantly flail me, you've taken time to know my moods, my habits, even my expressions." He reached out and lightly brushed the knuckles of one hand against the curve of her cheek. "A woman doesn't make a habit of studying a man she's indifferent to, Megan."

"So? I'm not indifferent." She shrugged, striving for a modicum of poise against him, his nearness, and his touch. "I don't like seeing you dupe my family. They're very much a part of the establishment that you resent, Rhys. There was love in this house between my parents, and there's still love for each of us kids."

"How did we get on the subject of love and kids?" he rasped darkly.

"*We* aren't, you lumbering fool." She leaned toward him and hissed in a hoarse undertone. "I was merely making a point. The thrust of which is you're a lousy bastard to waltz in here and look down your considerable nose at decent people who've done nothing to you except extend you the hospitality of their home."

"I'm beginning to wonder if I'm the only one with problems when it comes to trusting people."

"Megan!" exclaimed a loud, friendly voice, interrupting what probably would been another classic battle between Megan and Rhys.

She jerked around to see Ted Laird, whose family lived next door, bearing down on her. His arms were outstretched and a grin from ear to ear split his ugly but lovable face. Before she knew what was happening, Ted had bent down and swept her up in a giant hug.

"I knew you couldn't stay away indefinitely," he boomed in a voice guaranteed to do irreputable harm to eardrums and shatter delicate crystal. "It's my handsome mug that's got you hooked, isn't it? All the women are wild about it."

To her chagrin, Megan saw that she and Ted were the center of attention. Her brothers were encouraging his outrageous antics. And knowing their propensity for practical jokes, she wouldn't put it past them to have given Ted a call.

"Believe me, Ted," she said laughingly in spite of the trick she knew had been played on her, "you'll always occupy a *large* place in my memories." She stood on tiptoes and kissed him on the cheek. "It's good to see you."

"Same here, brat." He draped one hamlike arm across her shoulder and squeezed her, then turned to Rhys, who'd been observing the reunion with an outward calm that only Megan recognized as the prelude to an explosion.

Ted stepped toward him and extended his hand. "I'm Ted Laird. I hope you won't misunderstand that little act, but I've waited years to get Miss Priss back. She made my life miserable the summer I was sixteen. I'd managed to finally get a date with what I thought was an angel, and this bothersome minx hid in the hedge and giggled when she caught us necking."

For one tense moment Megan stood breathless, sensing the powerful surge of hatred emanating from Rhys. Then, as easily as he'd allowed himself to become absorbed into her family, he grasped Ted's hand.

"Rhys Warner. I can see your point," he said calmly. "She does have that unique ability to make one want to get back at her, doesn't she?"

"I can see you've already been the object of her sense of humor," Ted enthused, oblivious to Rhys's inner hatred of him. "If you find you can't handle her, just give me a call. I can fill you in on a number of interesting little escapades that will make her like putty in your hands."

"I'll certainly remember that, Ted," Rhys re-

151

marked in such friendly fashion, Megan wanted to belt him.

Rather than allow her another go at his tough hide, Rhys smiled sweetly at Megan, then walked with Ted over to where Ian was pouring out another round of Aunt Bea's homemade wine.

Megan silently fussed and fumed. But each attempt she made to be alone with Rhys was innocently or skillfully, she wasn't sure which, scotched by him or some member of her family.

She finally gave up and settled down for an enjoyable chat with her father. There would be another day to trim Mr. Warner's sails, she promised herself, and trim them she would!

CHAPTER NINE

By the time Megan returned to Pensacola on late Wednesday, she was emotionally worn out. She'd thrown herself into the proposal for Meta Electronics, then later, the lengthy meeting with Paul Chandler. That in itself was strain enough, without the added appearance of Rhys.

She wondered, as she went about the task of unpacking, where he was. She hadn't bothered asking his plans the evening before. Her anger had been too new, too easily ignited for a lengthy discussion. Apparently Rhys had had some doubts, for he also had appeared unusually quiet.

After putting away the last bit of clothing, she changed into a nightgown and robe, then carried the suitcase to the hall closet and stored it on the top shelf. Now for something to eat, she reminded herself, and set out for the kitchen.

Supper turned out to be a ham sandwich and a glass of iced tea. Megan carried both to the living room and over to the coffee table in front of the sofa. Before settling down, she picked up the TV listings and quickly checked the programing for the evening.

There was a choice of reruns, a western, and a blood-curdling mystery. She chose the mystery. Perhaps struggling to figure out the complicated plot would help keep her mind off Rhys. She knew she didn't want to see him, talk to him, or think about him—at least for this evening.

The sandwich had long since been eaten and the glass held nothing but the melting remains of the ice cubes. The heroine on the TV screen was crawling along a workman's scaffold fifteen stories up, the crazed murderer, who just happened to be her husband, in steady, surefooted pursuit.

Megan was sitting on the edge of the sofa, her arms tightly clutched about her upper body, her eyes literally glued to the screen. She was crawling every inch with the frightened woman, feeling every breath of tension that pierced her lungs.

The distraught heroine mercifully reached the edge of a section of solid flooring. She threw a panicked glance over her shoulder. Not seeing her husband, she heaved a gasping sigh of relief. She'd beaten him!

She turned back, one hand outstretched to grasp the solidness of the platform. But instead of wood, she felt human skin . . . and bone, covered by cloth.

154

Stunned eyes crept upward inch by paralyzed inch over leg, thigh, and torso, to stare with renewed horror into a pair of fanatical eyes. She opened her mouth and screamed, the sound piercing the air the same instant a heavy knocking sounded at Megan's door.

Giving a visible start that sent her knee banging into the sharp edge of the table, Megan charged to her feet, the fingers of fear surging throughout her body like quicksilver.

She stood in a momentary state of confusion, still caught in the throes of the mystery, and unable to separate fact from reality. When the knock came again, more insistently, she pressed her palms to her midriff, relief replacing fear, and hurried to the door.

She opened it and found Rhys standing with a hand on either side of the doorjamb, a heavy scowl masking his face.

"It sounds like your friend Ted followed you to Pensacola and was in hot pursuit around the sofa." He looked tired, the signs of weariness and fatigue clearly stamped in the harsh lines of his face. What on earth had he been doing for the last twenty-four hours?

"Unfortunately Ted was unavailable," she said cuttingly, stepping back and waving him in. "I'm counting the days till he can join me. Now that we've dealt with your usual insult, perhaps you'll tell me why you've bothered stopping by?"

Rhys raised one hand and tugged at the knot of his tie, loosening it, his dark gaze narrowed in silent appraisal as he watched her. "Believe me, if I knew the answer to that question, I'd be more than happy to share it with you." Without asking permission, he calmly removed the dark gray suit jacket and tossed it, along with his tie, toward a chair.

"*Do* make yourself comfortable," Megan said goadingly, then abruptly swung about and marched back to where she'd been sitting on the sofa. Damn him! She wasn't ready to see him. She'd given in to his request to meet her family, only to be forced to stand by and watch him make a mockery of everything she believed in.

Nothing in her past—from childhood to present—had prepared her for the single-minded loneliness of this man, a loneliness fed by his deep-seated suspicion of people, especially women.

She thought back to the evening before and remembered the flashes of longing she'd seen reflected in his eyes as they followed the laughing antics of her family, only to see the same lingering be replaced by a brittle grimness.

It was like watching a small boy standing on the sidelines, waiting for some encouragement, some small hint from the others that he was wanted. When the invitation wasn't extended, the little boy would absorb the silent hurt and rejection by adding an additional layer of bravado to hide his disappointment as he waited for the next slap from fate.

In Rhys's case the small boy had been successful in attaining and in achieving materialistically. He'd done so, however, without one vital part of him intact—a heart. Not the organ that pumped blood through his veins, but the heart that generates love, nourishes it, and finally offers it as a gift to another person.

It was the clinking of ice as it fell into a glass that broke into Megan's thoughtful mood. She looked up just as Rhys came from the kitchen, the glass in his hand containing a generous portion of scotch.

"I hope you don't mind," he remarked coolly, his eyes searching her face. "But you did seem to be involved in some sort of personal battle."

Megan met his stare with her own uncertain one, wishing it was a simple matter of telling him to get lost, go away, or some other equally insulting remark. Instead, she shrugged. Why pretend an indifference they both knew would be a lie?

"Have you eaten?" The question was asked with a spontaneity clearly at odds with any revenge she might have debated upon.

"Yes," he said quietly as he dropped beside her, then let his head rest against the back of the sofa. "I had dinner on the plane."

"The plane?" Megan asked disbelievingly. "From Atlanta to Pensacola?"

"From Denver to Dallas, then on to Pensacola. I flew out of Atlanta around midnight last night."

"Have you had any sleep?"

"Not more than four or five hours in the last thirty-six. It's not unusual though. I'm always

157

keyed up when I'm closing out a deal." He gave her a flinty-eyed grin. "Adding substantial amounts of gold to my coffers always makes me a bit hyper."

"If your present condition is any indication," she said crisply, "it also leaves you looking as though you've been through a battle."

No wonder the first thing she'd noticed was how tired he looked. He was pushing himself like a machine. But even machines, in spite of being constructed of steel, were known to break down.

"I'd think by now you'd have enough 'gold' stashed away to satisfy even the greediest person. According to the articles I read regarding you and your organization, your assests reached the vulgar stage several years ago."

"Ah, but now they're positively obscene, Miss Colby. Doesn't that shock your middle-class values?" he teased, and somehow Megan couldn't find it in her to be angry any longer. She felt her hand nearest him being engulfed in his strong grasp and wondered, fleetingly, at his unconscious habit of wanting to always touch her. It was a far cry from his projection of himself as a cold, unfeeling person.

"One can't change the entire world, Mr. Warner," she softly murmured. "So . . ." She settled back comfortably, not bothering to brace her body against his heavier weight on the cushions that caused her to inch closer and closer to his inviting warmth. "One must learn other more subtle ways of achieving her goals."

"And exactly what are your goals, princess?" he asked, turning slightly so that Megan found herself pressed solidly into his chest, the scent of him settling over her like a welcome release from the doubts and fears plaguing her. She felt the vibration of his deep voice as it rumbled and forced its way from his chest and found some inexplicable excitement in such an insignificant happening.

A gentle smile, brought on by their bodies touching, as much as the quiet verbal sparring they were becoming involved in, tugged at her lips. "A girl, Rhys, is taught from the cradle to be mysterious, profound. We learn, thanks to the overall scheme of things, to become proficient at beguilement, seduction, and flirtatious maneuvers. After accomplishing all that by age six, do you honestly expect us to suddenly open up and reveal all?"

"To me, yes," he answered ruthlessly, his palm finding its way beneath her robe to cup the pivotal point of her shoulder. "I'll be damned if I know what there is about you that gets to me, but you do. You stay with me day and night, you witch. I'm jealous as hell of your friends, your family, and I could have killed 'friendly' Ted."

"And you find this . . . attachment for me to be objectionable?" Megan whispered, in her mind thanking the gods responsible for this sudden burst of confession from him. Was he really falling? Was it possible for him to feel the emotional need of a commitment between a man and woman? "Do you resent the fact that there's something about me that keeps digging at you?"

"Hell, yes," he grinned halfheartedly. "I also have spent years perfecting my craft, Miss Colby. It's gotten me through some sticky situations when certain members of your sex decided I'd be the perfect fixture in their future." He paused, letting his gaze slowly touch each feature of her face, the expression in his dark depths so intense, so bold, Megan felt a shiver of desire scamper over her as if his lips had touched each spot his eyes had lingered upon.

"Are *you*, by any chance, planning on trying to nail my infamous hide to your cabin door, Miss Colby?"

Megan watched him through the sun-tipped thickness of her lashes and felt the strength of his hand on her body and debated the rationale of her next move. Dare she follow her heart or continue to remain safely on the fringes of life?

"I do hate to appear boastful, Mr. Warner, nor do I care to be lumped with the previous women in your life, but the answer is yes."

"Many before you have tried and failed."

"Oh . . ." she teased. "But they were lacking one powerful ingredient."

"Which is?"

"You'll learn in time."

"I'm not the marrying kind."

"I don't recall asking you."

"Longstanding arrangements cause me to

160

break out in hives and immediately seek safer territory."

"Longstanding conjures up thoughts of weeks . . . months," she patiently explained, looking him straight in the eye. "You flatter yourself. My plans can be carried out in a matter of days."

"Are you presenting me with a challenge, or warning me?"

"Neither. I'm merely stating a fact." She allowed the fingers of one hand to tiptoe across his chest to the buttons of his shirt, then slowly, boldly, she undid the first one . . . the second, then the rest. "It's time, Mr. Warner, that a *woman* take you in hand. I've grown extremely weary of this attitude of yours where females are concerned. Only a mouse packs his tent and silently steals away in the middle of the night. A man stays to see what the daylight will bring. Are you a man or a mouse, Mr. Warner?" she whispered provocatively, letting the pink tip of her tongue slowly moisten the smooth fullness of her lips.

The reaction from Rhys was instantaneous and explosive, as Megan hoped it would be. His mouth took hers greedily, the extension of his passion forging an invisible bridge between them, an intangible force that rocked Megan to her very toes as she opened her heart, her mouth, her very being to him.

Their tongues darted and teased, then caressed each other hungrily, as though all prior restrictions so much in evidence in their previous meetings had been swept away.

161

Their hands, anxious for the feel of flesh against flesh, carelessly pushed aside clothing, unmindful of the thin, fragile straps of a gown or the quiet snap of a button on the front of a shirt. Desire that had been smoldering between them for days was now ignited into a rushing inferno of need that could no longer be put off.

Rhys's lips inched their way down a softly arched neck, pearlescent in the soft glow of the lamp, to creamy breasts laid bare to the velvety caress of his gaze. The excited tips were rosy-pink and became a perfect morsel around which his tongue circled and teased till Megan groaned from the painful pleasure snaking its way in and out and around each sensitive part of her.

Her emotional self, as well as her physical being, was reacting in a wild, frenzied manner. His gentleness—for he was so very gentle—brought tears to her eyes, while physical needs within her were demanding more and more of him.

When he stripped the gown and robe completely from her and brushed it carelessly over the edge of the cushion, Megan opened blue eyes brilliant with desire. And though her glasses had been lost somewhere in the shuffle, she didn't need sight to recognize the wonder in Rhys's expression as he stared at her body.

"You're so very lovely," he murmured against the skin at her waist. "But these will have to go." His thumbs slid beneath the lacy band of her beige briefs and eased them down over shapely hips and thighs and lastly her feet.

Before he could resume his special brand of torment, Megan grabbed at one side of his shirt still hanging from his shoulders and tugged.

Rhys saw what she was trying to do and helped her. In moments he was bare from the waist up.

Again she placed a restraining hand between them when he bent toward her. He frowned, his powerful arms bracing him above her, that haunted look briefly surfacing in his eyes. "This is no time to get cold feet, princess," he muttered.

"I would hardly call the state of my undress as befitting a shy, retiring maiden, would you? What I'm trying to accomplish, you impossible idiot, is to get you out of these pants." She grinned so enchantingly at him that Rhys closed his eyes for a moment and dropped his head, his crisp, dark hair tickling the softness of her breasts.

"You frighten the hell out of me, do you know that?" he asked as he raised his head and stared down at her.

"I sort of got that impression when you turned deathly pale and began gasping for breath," she said matter-of-factly, her fingers finding and working at the waistband of his pants.

"Don't tease, princess," Rhys rasped as he took over the job himself and was soon as naked as she.

Instead of letting her gaze linger on his body, lazily studying each and every part of him, Megan opened her arms to the tall, frowning man standing proud before her. "I assure you, I've never been more serious in my entire life." There

163

would be time enough later to gather other interesting bits of information to use against him.

Rhys chuckled at her brazeness, then bent and lifted her in his arms. "Your sofa is nice, but it cramps my style, Miss Colby," he whispered against her ear as he made his way to the bedroom.

Megan offered no reply. Her thoughts were taken over with the spreading eddies of arousal surrounding her. For with each step Rhys took, her breast brushed against the wiry growth that covered his chest. She looked down, her fuzzy gaze pinned by the sight of one proud, pink nipple snuggled warm and cozy amid the sea of black.

When Rhys stopped at the bed, he placed her on her back, his own tanned body following. They turned to each other, touching, tasting. Not only was Megan receiving gratification from his hands that were sweeping her, from fingers learning the secrets of her body, she was also attempting to transmit a message of love and need and desire.

Where she'd never before consciously dwelled on wanting to explore a man's body, now she did. Her fingers kneaded the muscles of his neck and shoulders, then slipped lower to brush against his back, enlarging her scope of play to include bold forays across one hip to his stomach. She boldly outlined his navel, the circle widening each time till that part of him that was the counterpart of her own femininity rested beneath her touch.

164

The rush of air that swooshed from Rhys's lungs brought a thrill to her as well as an awareness heretofore unheard of. She was capable of meeting his needs, of giving him sexual completeness as well as receiving it. And for all his macho image, Rhys Warner needed a woman's gentle touch, her caress—to make him a whole man.

"Kiss me, princess," Rhys demanded.

She did, then gasped as she felt herself being turned onto her back. Other noises from her broke the hushed silence in the room as his firm, sure fingers traced flirting patterns along the insides of her thighs, her back, and over every inch of her. His mouth seemed equally addicted to the taste of her as his lips nipped and grazed the tender outer sides of her breasts. When he moved lower and began to work his way from her toes upward, Megan clutched wildly at his shoulders, her fingers burrowing beneath his black hair to follow the shape of his head, urging him upward in his total possession of her body.

He was no longer a man ruled by distrust and suspicion, but a lover. This wasn't one of the faceless women from his past, but his own special witch. For surely only a witch could weave the spell of wanting, of needing, as subtly as she'd done.

Suddenly the taste of her, the feel of her writhing body beneath his hands wasn't enough. He wanted to possess her, become a part of her. For only then could he exorcise her hold on him.

His firm hands snaked upward over her golden body as his bronze knee parted her silky-smooth thighs.

Megan arched to meet him, the core of her being taking him, completing the joining of their bodies.

He dictated, she followed. He challenged, she surrendered. On and on it went, this wildfire that licked at them, in a world of unreality that cushioned them against the wild and strange elements, then just as brutally tossed them headlong into another climactic swirl of passion.

Then slowly, and with incredible gentleness, Megan felt herself floating, her entire being suffused in a warm glow. She was relaxed to the extent that her arms and legs were like dead weights.

Her last dream-warped recollection was of Rhys braced above her, the fuzzy outline of his features immobile as he stared at her. "So beautiful," she murmured drowsily, turning her head so that her lips brushed his outstretched hand that was supporting him. "So beautiful."

It was the sound of low-voiced conversation coming from the television that no one had thought to turn off that awakened Megan. That and the unfamiliar weight of a small tree laying across her chest. She went to move her legs, and found them similarly restricted.

"I was beginning to think you'd never wake

166

up," an amused voice cleared the last remnants of sleep-induced fog from her brain.

She turned her head and found herself looking into Rhys's face—only an inch or two separating them. A slow, tentative smile pulled at her lips. "It isn't nice to watch a person sleep," she told him. "It's like, like a peeping Tom, peering into windows."

"Funny," he rasped huskily, "but I don't feel the slightest bit ashamed."

"That's because you have no shame," Megan frowned owlishly, wishing she could see him in the dim light that shone from the living room. "You seduced a poor innocent woman without even buying her dinner. No sirree, no shame at all."

"None whatsoever," he agreed. "In fact, I've been lying here holding you, wondering what big guns you'll draw on me next."

"Scared?"

"No," he drawled huskily, "not scared. More . . . cautious. I've always made a point of knowing what the opposition was planning. Whereas with you, I feel like I've been sucked up in the middle of a tornado."

"Beast!" she exclaimed playfully, tapping him on the chin. "Does it bother you to learn you can't always control everything in your life?"

"That, my beguiling witch, is exactly what I'm asking myself. I'm not used to sharing my thoughts, myself with another person. Yet, when I'm with you, I find I do just that."

Megan knew he hadn't changed his thinking, but at least she had gotten him to begin questioning his own motives and ideas. And somehow she knew she must be content with that small victory for now.

For in their lovemaking she'd seen him at his most vulnerable, and at his strongest. Never for a second had he forgotten her. He'd shepherded her from the peaks of passion, through the valleys and back to the peaks again and again, his arms safely guarding and protecting her.

Rhys Warner was a man of deep, intense caring and feeling, and Megan Colby made a promise to herself that all that caring and feeling would belong to her. Poor Rhys. He might chafe and strain against the noose as it began to tighten, but Megan had an idea she knew exactly the way to soothe his fears. In fact, she thought as she gave a luxurious stretch of her body and smiled, now would be the perfect moment to begin her lover's education in becoming a model husband.

For once she was glad she couldn't see the actual expression that rushed to and became mirrored in his dark eyes as she began a delightful game of tracing feathery patterns on his taut stomach and thighs.

"What the hell are you up to, Megan?" Rhys asked gruffly, his voice cracking slightly as he sucked in his breath in anticipation of her hand arriving at that part of him that was now awake and eager to do her bidding.

"I'm going to make love to you, sweetheart.

I'm going to do everything to you that I've been reading about since I was twelve years old and started stealing my brothers' . . . er . . . literature."

"Then heaven help me," he groaned.

"True."

CHAPTER TEN

The next morning found Megan outwardly the same, if one discounted the added sparkle in her eyes and the rosy glow of her cheeks.

Inwardly she wondered if the tension that flowed just beneath the surface was anything compared to what a gambler must feel when the stakes were high and only one more card would determine if he won or lost.

As she sat at her desk attempting to plow through the work that had piled up in her absence, she was unable to keep back the events of the evening before. Would her plan work? Could she, by asking nothing of Rhys, by even appearing at times to be indifferent, break down the barrier he'd built around himself?

Finding and falling in love with a man of her dreams usually figured in every woman's future,

Megan quietly reflected. But finding that man and falling in love, only to have to hide that same love, was frustrating.

She had no difficulty at all in visualizing Rhys's expression, were she foolish enough to blurt out her deepest feelings for him. "He'd make a road-runner look like he was standing still," she remarked crossly. She stared thoughtfully into space for a few more minutes, then nodded. "I definitely think it's time for the indifferent approach. If hot pursuit sends him packing, then let's see what cool indifference will do."

In the middle of the morning Katie came in with some additional mail. She laid it on Megan's desk, then walked over and stared out the window at the overcast skies that had dumped showers since daybreak.

"Have you ever been in a hurricane, Megan?"

"Once," Megan replied as she scanned the mail. "Why?"

"Well, from the looks of things, the storm that's brewing could easily change directions and come ashore here."

"It could, I suppose, but it's not likely to happen."

"It's happened before," Katie maintained stubbornly.

"I'm sure it has," Megan agreed. "But Ned Carey called about an hour ago and told me we wouldn't need to worry about setting up the emergency shelters this evening as planned. Hurricane Toni had been downgraded to a tropical depression. The most we are likely to get is a continuation of our present weather for a couple of days." She smiled. "Does that make you feel better?"

"Yes," Katie sighed, exhaling a huge breath of relief.

"Are you seeing John this evening?"

"Naturally," the pert brunette replied, a smile replacing the frown. "We're invited to a party."

"Sounds like fun."

"I've some other news as well," Katie informed her. "John has been asked to join the staff of one of the local clinics. That means our wedding date, which has become a joke, could actually be within the next six weeks."

"Oh, Katie." Megan smiled. "Has John definitely decided to accept the offer?"

"Yes. For a while there I had my doubts. He was so gung-ho on making it on his own. But what with the cost of equipment being what it is, plus drugs and overhead, I think he's finally faced the hard facts of life."

"If it means the two of you can be married soon, I'm sure he won't mind the change."

"He'd better not," Katie said determinedly, at which Megan laughed.

How lucky the two of them were, Megan later thought after Katie left the room. There didn't appear to be any complications other than financial ones, which would be eliminated for the most part by John's move.

If only her own problem with Rhys could be so

easily settled. Where Katie and John found the lack of money to be a large factor in their not being able to marry, Rhys's wealth had, in part, caused him to become suspicious of the most innocent overtures extended him.

As the afternoon wore on, Megan lost the sparkle, the glow, that had brightened her cheeks earlier. She hadn't heard a word from Rhys. He was certainly under no obligation to her just because they'd gone to bed together. And, if she were completely honest with herself, she couldn't deny that she'd been looking for exactly this sort of reaction from him.

He'd admitted, grudgingly so, that he found her attractive, enjoyed being with her, and was unable to dismiss her from his mind. Any one of these feelings regarding a woman was enough to cause his black heart to beat faint. But having all three channeled toward one scheming female was obviously proving to be more than he could take.

Megan had no trouble at all imagining him in a sheikh's robes, skulking about the Sahara. No, she quietly decided, waiting for Rhys at this stage of their relationship was really all she could do. She'd made her decision, and her only comfort was in the love she carried in her heart for him.

Why did this affliction, this sickness called love, have to be so painful? Was there some ancient and mysterious law that decreed all lovers must spend a certain amount of time suffering?

* * *

Walking into her apartment after work was like coming face to face with her tormentor. Everyplace she looked she could see him. Sprawled on the sofa, in the chair. Even the kitchen wasn't safe from his memory.

When she entered the bedroom she was almost positive she could still smell his scent, and for a moment tears gathered behind her glasses, blurring her vision.

"Stop it!" she scolded herself. "Just stop thinking about him." And with all her might, she tried.

After eating a salad, then changing into a comfortable pair of slacks and a baggy T-shirt, Megan decided to tackle one of those jobs she'd put off indefinitely. On this particular evening she chose to straighten and clean the kitchen drawers.

It wasn't exhausting work, nor was it the most stimulating venture she'd been involved in. But it kept her hands busy. When it ended, however, she found it to be still relatively early. She washed her hands, dried them on a paper towel, then switched off the light and left the kitchen. Perhaps television could help fill the void for an hour or so.

Megan was almost to the sofa when the knock came. She froze in her tracks! Rhys was the only person she knew who knocked. Everyone else used the doorbell.

Should she answer or should she pretend to be gone? Wouldn't it better serve her purpose to be less accessible?

But even as she was asking herself these questions, she was starting toward the door. Playing hard to get might have its usefulness, but when your heart was breaking for the sight of a particular man and your arms were aching for the feel of him, then the basic feminine means of entrapment didn't seem nearly as attractive.

Opening the door was the hardest thing Megan had ever done. The night before she'd channeled all her love for Rhys into each caress of her fingertips, in the feel of her lips, in the way her body welcomed him. What she wasn't allowed to say out loud had been spoken through body language. Had it been enough?

There was no overt change in his appearance other than a haunted look in his gaze and the tiny network of lines at the corners of his eyes that were more pronounced. His expression was that of one in the throes of severe pain. He pushed back from his leaning position and met her inquiring look.

"May I come in?" he asked with the cool politeness of a stranger.

"Certainly," she said, suppressing the insane urge to giggle at his polite frostiness.

"May I get you a drink?" she finally asked. He'd ignored the sofa and chairs, and was doggedly pacing the confines of her living room.

"Scotch," floated over his shoulder without a break in his stride.

Megan shook her head disbelievingly, then turned and left the room. He is a basket case, she decided as she took down a glass, then added

175

scotch and two cubes of ice. Wasn't it strange that women had always been thought of as the weaker sex?

She returned to the living room and carried the drink over to him. Rhys paused by the glass doors that opened onto the tiny patio adjoining the apartment. The drapes were pulled back and he was staring into the rain-streaked night, a dark, brooding expression on his face.

Megan hesitated before breaking into his thoughts. Finally she could put it off no longer. Anything was better than the awful mood he was in. She touched his arm, then handed him the drink.

Not only did he take the glass in his large grasp, but he took her hand as well. He placed the drink on a small table by the glass doors, then drew a surprised Megan to him until she was leaning back against his chest and his arms were tight around her.

"I deliberately didn't call you today." His breath was hot on her neck as his lips and tongue nibbled and tasted.

"I know."

"Did that bother you?"

"Did you want it to?"

"Yes, but *only* bother. Not to hurt you."

"You accomplished both."

"Will you forgive me if I'm not sorry?"

"Of course. Your pride is at stake."

"Why so generous?"

"The victor shouldn't brag about winning the battle."

"Are you so certain you've won?"

"You're here, aren't you?"

"What if it's only for this once?"

"Is it?"

The silence was deafening. Megan could almost feel the struggle going on inside him, could almost hear the silent arguing of an old, ingrained suspicion fighting against the deep honesty of love. A love that was offered, not in exchange for something, but freely.

"No, witch," he said on a shuddered breath. "It's for keeps."

"Afraid?"

"Terrified."

Megan slowly turned in his arms, her eyes like glowing sapphires. She raised her hands and framed his face, drinking in the sight of him. "What exactly are you afraid of, Rhys?"

"That you'll stop loving me." For a brief moment an incredible sadness flashed across his face. "That marriage will lose its appeal after a while."

Megan used her thumbs to smooth away the tautness of his cheeks, to ease the rigid slash of his mouth.

"Why don't we leave marriage out of it, Rhys? Why don't we live together instead? There'll be no strings for either of us."

"What about your family?" he asked, looking faintly shocked.

"What about them?"

"You told me about the incident with Michael Kline. I hardly think they've changed, do you?"

"So? Even though we're close, we lead separate lives. I haven't needed their permission for a number of years."

"Well, I don't like it," he stated ominously, reaching up and grasping her wrists. He brought them to rest on his chest, then slipped his arms back around her. "I don't like the idea of you being in a position for people to gossip. I think we'd best settle the whole thing by getting married."

"My, my." Megan smiled. "You sound so positive."

"I am positive. Positive that I love you. Positive that it's hell being away from you. That only leaves one thing, doesn't it?"

"I'm afraid so, Mr. Warner." She tried so hard to be humble.

"You've known it would end like this all along, haven't you?" he demanded, his dark eyes devouring her in spite of the scowl.

"I hoped—dreamed. I was even ready to indulge in all sorts of underhanded tricks to entrap you. I've grown quite shameless where you are concerned."

"How shameless?" he asked seductively, his hands lightly running up and down her body, awakening her senses to a familiar but new awareness.

"Are you challenging me?" she prompted.

"Yes."

"In that case . . ." she casually remarked, then stepped back and reached for the cord that closed the draperies and pulled it. Next she crossed the few feet to one end of the sofa and switched off the lamp. The only other light came from the bathroom.

She turned and held out her hand to him. Rhys caught it and followed.

There was just enough light in the bedroom to see outlines of faces and figures, but not detailed features. Megan turned when she reached the bed and, without hesitation, began undressing him.

First to go was his coat and tie. Next she worked on the shirt, slipping the buttons from their narrow openings. She tugged the tail of the shirt from his pants and pushed it off his shoulders. With one quick move of her hand, the belt on his pants was opened, and the zipper eased down.

Soon Rhys stood before her, tall and large and powerful. He was totally masculine without being overpowering. He exuded a sexuality that in no way infringed upon his masculinity. In fact, to Megan, he was perfect.

As though aware of her feelings at the moment, Rhys deftly slipped the shirt she was wearing over her head. Before disrobing her further, he cupped the soft weight of her breasts in his palms, then lowered his head to nuzzle the fragrant nectar.

"You're so lovely," he groaned, inhaling the scent of her. He was hungry for her, on fire for her, and her soft, sweet love that had surrounded and held him in its grip.

With a shuddering sigh ripping the air from his lungs, Rhys interrupted the torture he was administering to himself to remove Megan's slacks and panties. When they both stood naked, they went into each other's arms and fell to the softness of the bed.

There was an urgency on both their parts as they touched that hadn't been present before. It seemed imperative that they pledge, by the joining of their bodies, their undying love for each other.

To Megan, it was her first opportunity to express openly her love, her compassion for this lonely man. He lent strength to her life as she'd never known. They each had voids that only the other could fill—two halves that were whole now.

She gave a pleasured sigh as firm hands began stroking the softness of her hips and buttocks, slowly inching their way up over her back and shoulders to cup each side of her face. "I love you, Megan Colby. Everything I have or am is yours. And God help us both if you ever get tired of me."

Megan heard the unspoken pleading in his voice. But mere words at this stage would never reassure him. Faith and trust would come, she'd see to that. In the meantime she opened her arms to him.

* * *

Megan stood back and stared critically at the table. The flowers and candles looked perfect, as they had the last ten times she'd checked them.

It was exactly six months to the day that she had become Mrs. Rhys Warner. This evening was to be their very first, special anniversary.

She'd cooked all his favorite dishes, was wearing his favorite blue dress, and was playing his favorite music.

Not that Rhys was a difficult husband; he wasn't. In fact, he'd made tremendous progress as far as his jealousy was concerned. He no longer considered the guests at the dinner parties Megan gave as being parasites, and had actually come to be friends with several men other than Jack.

Her family was still somewhat of a problem though. When the clan was together they demanded a certain amount of Megan's time. That Rhys didn't like. But as with all wily characters who've lived and survived by their wits and instincts, he was adapting.

One of his staunchest supporters was Amelia Wrafton. Rhys had given the land on Spencer Street to the historical society and the ladies were ecstatic.

In another few months, Megan felt certain she would have to take a leave of absence from her job to have her baby.

Although, when she would tell Rhys she was pregnant he might insist that she resign sooner.

He might also be angry when he heard her news, he'd . . . he'd . . . She tried to stop tormenting herself. Men became fathers every second of every day. Surely Rhys wasn't so juvenile that he would resent his own child. And yet, he'd seemed pleased when he learned she was taking birth control pills. She didn't bother to tell him that she'd discontinued the pills in hopes of getting pregnant.

The sound of the key in the front door caught Megan's ear. She turned and flew to the kitchen, then stood uncertainly in the middle of the room. The slam of the door was heard, then the muffled tread of Rhys's footsteps through the corridor and across the living room. She heard him call her name. She hesitated, her breathing reduced to short, quick breaths.

Before she could decide the best course of action to follow, Rhys came barreling through the doorway. For the tiniest fraction of a second she saw panic in his eyes.

"You didn't answer," he said simply.

"I was finishing up dinner." Megan smiled as she walked over to him. She stood on tiptoe and kissed him. When she would have stepped back, Rhys caught her close, his arms locking about her.

"I was afraid you—"

"Don't." Megan smiled, shushing him by placing a forefinger against his lips. "We're far beyond that stage now, don't you agree?"

"Most of the time," he grinned crookedly.

"Only occasionally do old fears and doubts come back to haunt me."

"Are you hungry?"

"Hungry?" he asked, almost blinking at how quickly she changed the subject.

"For dinner," she said crisply. "We are celebrating our anniversary, or have you forgotten?"

"No, ma'am." Rhys was quick to defend himself. "In fact"—he reached in an inside pocket of his jacket and withdrew a long, narrow, silver-wrapped package—"I just happen to have picked up this little bauble on my lunch hour." He cocked his head to one side and looked at the package on both sides. "What do you suppose it is?"

"It had better be for me," Megan grinned, then made a quick swipe with one hand and immediately began to tear open the paper. She gave a gasp of pleasure at the lovely diamond pendant, set in a lacy web of delicate filigree, suspended from a slender, gold chain.

"It's beautiful, Rhys, but you really shouldn't have. My jewelry collection is growing at a rapid pace."

"And you really aren't that wild about it, are you?"

"It's beautiful, and I'm flattered that you think of me so often, but I'm just as happy when you walk through that door each evening. Is that so hard to believe?"

"Six months ago it would have been. Now," he smiled, "I understand it perfectly. But you'll have

183

to learn to deal with my gifts, because I enjoy buying things for you."

"I promise to always show proper appreciation. Now," she attempted to get the conversation back to the subject of dinner, "let's eat."

She leaned past Rhys and grabbed two oven mitts, opened the oven, then removed the oyster casserole.

"What is this preoccupation you have with food, Mrs. Warner? Are you attempting to butter me up before you tell me you've wrecked your new car?"

Megan remained turned away from him, busying herself with adding the two salads and the flaky rolls to the tray. There was no need putting it off any longer. With her nervousness and his sharp eye, he'd have it out of her in five minutes anyway.

"I didn't wreck my car, Rhys, but I am pregnant. Do you want Roquefort or oil and vinegar dressing on your salad?"

"Oil and vin . . ." His voice trailed off, only to regain its strength. "Pregnant?" he boomed incredulously. "How?"

"The obvious way, I assure you." Megan turned and stared just as curiously at her husband. "Are you angry, Rhys?"

"Angry?" he thundered in such a forceful manner Megan actually jumped. "My God, princess." He closed his eyes and slowly shook his dark head. "Is that why you've been as nervous as a cat in a roomful of rocking chairs? Did you really think I would be jealous of my own child?"

"It . . . did occur to me," she admitted somewhat shamefully now that she saw the excitement in his eyes.

Any thoughts of regret she might be feeling, however, would have to be put on hold, for at that moment Rhys plucked her from the floor and swung her high in the air, before setting her on the counter and placing his hands on either side of her.

"I'm thrilled . . . ecstatic . . . overjoyed . . . okay?" And Megan believed him. "Now tell me when?"

"In six months."

"And your job?"

"I'll take a leave of absence when the baby comes and then we'll play it by ear. Okay?"

"I think I can live with that." He caught her face in his hands, the love shining out to her from his gaze, bringing tears to her eyes. "You never cease to amaze me, Megan Warner. You learned to love a grouchy old cynic like me, took a chance by marrying me, and now you're going to give me a child. You're my life, princess, my talisman."

"I love you, Rhys Warner," she whispered. "Now and throughout eternity."

Without another word he lifted her in his arms. "I hope the food won't spoil."

"So do I," she smiled knowingly. "But if it does, we can always order a pizza. Right now I'd rather be in my husband's arms."

185

"How nice, my dear. For that's exactly what's about to happen," he told her as he left the kitchen and headed straight for the bedroom.

"Happy anniversary, Rhys."

"Happy anniversary, princess."

All-new
Candlelight
Newsletter

**An exceptional,
free offer awaits readers
of Dell's incomparable Candlelight Ecstasy and Supreme Romances.**

Subscribe to our all-new CANDLELIGHT NEWSLETTER and you will receive—at absolutely no cost to you—exciting, exclusive information about today's finest romance novels and novelists. You'll be part of a select group to receive sneak previews of upcoming Candlelight Romances, well in advance of publication.

You'll also go behind the scenes to "meet" our Ecstasy and Supreme authors, learning firsthand where they get their ideas and how they made it to the top. News of author appearances and events will be detailed, as well. And contributions from the Candlelight editor will give you the inside scoop on how she makes her decisions about what to publish—and how *you* can try your hand at writing an Ecstasy or Supreme.

You'll find all this and more in Dell's CANDLELIGHT NEWSLETTER. And best of all, *it costs you nothing*. That's right! It's Dell's way of thanking our loyal Candlelight readers and of adding another dimension to your reading enjoyment.

Just fill out the coupon below, return it to us, and look forward to receiving the first of many CANDLELIGHT NEWS-LETTERS—overflowing with the kind of excitement that only enhances our romances!

Return to: DELL PUBLISHING CO., INC.   B216D
      Candlelight Newsletter • Publicity Department
      245 East 47 Street • New York, N.Y. 10017

Name_____

Address_____

City_____

State_____Zip_____

LOOK FOR NEXT MONTH'S
CANDLELIGHT ECSTASY ROMANCES ®

Candlelight Ecstasy Romances™

$1.95 each

CANDLELIGHT Ecstasy Supreme

Candlelight
Ecstasy Romances™

$1.95 each